MW01701816

DICK DOES LIBERIA

AVERY M. DICK

THE LARSON AGENCY
FAIRFAX, VIRGINIA

ISBN: 978-0-615-25468-5

CONTENTS

FOREWORD

Puns and other wordplay can lighten an otherwise sad story. That's the case here. A little levity was sometimes necessary to tell a story that was decidedly grim—perhaps just dark humor on the Dark Continent. Liberia was on a downward trajectory and had little chance of turning itself around. Hope and confidence were in short supply like everything else in the beleaguered country.

The entire population was suffering greatly and the government of Ellen Johnson-Sirleaf was largely helpless in the face of overwhelming obstacles. Rampant corruption, indifference and crushing poverty all conspired against breaking the death spiral. That's because a long, bloody civil war had drained the nation's resources and spirits. Now a human monster threatened her fragile regime and its democratic institutions. When it rained, it poured, especially in Liberia's wettest of rainy seasons.

There was only one potential bright spot on an otherwise bleak horizon—oil and natural gas. Huge fields had been discovered off the country's coast and in its territorial waters. The big energy companies were already licking their lips and calculating their outrageous profits. By the way, the prospective was good for a gusher. Unfortunately, Liberia was ripe for the picking and plucking given its weakened condition. The greedy vultures were already circling, flapping their wings and beating their puffed chests in anticipation of good things to come.

The monster had other plans for the nation that included his taking power by force, hook or crook or whatever means necessary. His appetite for money and absolute power was insatiable. He was a ravenous glutton whose hunger for more could never be sated. Equally alarming was his sociopathic bent for ruthless and reckless behavior. The unholy union of aberrant desires and brutally cold-blooded intentions spelled disaster for the frail country. Whatever the costs, he planned to topple Ellen Sirleaf and install himself as the next president of the fledgling republic.

My role in the drama was all too clear: bell the cat to prevent a coup and civil war. My employer of second-to-last resort, the State Department's Diplomatic Security Service, had ordered me to catch a monster while it was distracted or napping. I thought McDonald's was looking better and better by the moment. "How about some fries with the burger, ma'am?"

I hope you enjoy the read and say a little prayer for the Liberian people.

Very truly yours,
Avery M. Dick III (DS Special Agent, Ret.)

P.S. May God bless America!

CHAPTER 1

DANKEST AFRICA

"Phil, you need to remember that Liberians are wicked and vicious people."
—Ellen Johnson-Sirleaf, President, Republic of Liberia

The fasten seat belt sign flashed-on and the pilot announced we were approaching Roberts Field and to prepare for landing. The mostly black passengers and the few white expats onboard dutifully complied with the instruction. I suspected a number of people were returning home from the Diaspora after many years of self-imposed exile. Liberia was not a tourist destination by any stretch of the imagination. A positive, upbeat imagination and strong dose of hopefulness were necessary to emotionally cope with the current conditions in the desperately poor country. That was because Liberia was down on its prospects and almost down for the count. Its collective sanity and tenuous stability were quickly slipping away. Those who couldn't or wouldn't grasp the dire conditions and consequences of the situation were simply whistling past the graveyard. I quickly stifled a yawn and an uncontrollable urge to purse my lips.

As the plane turned on final approach, I saw it was raining

heavily, not surprising for the wet season that still had two months to go before the weather turned sunny and brutally hot. Regardless, it was always hot and humid here with the only relief offered by the intermittent breezes off the Atlantic. Monrovia had the distinction of being the rainiest capital in the world. I didn't bother to verify the claim because I didn't particularly care and forgotten to bring my hydrometer. In my particular profession, wet-work was always a possibility and an occupational hazard. Thank God I'd remembered to bring an umbrella and my rubbers!

The 30 mile trip from the airport to the city reminded me of my previous visit in 1992 when I served as acting Regional Security Officer at the U.S. embassy. Between then and now, the country had undergone 14 on-and-off again years of devastating civil war. The entire country was now in shambles and desperately trying to reestablish basic infrastructures. No commercial electricity existed in the country and other basic services and products were nonexistent, scarce or prohibitively expensive. Liberia was a basket case without even the pretense of a basket—wicker and rattan were in short supply too.

The United Nations, wealthy donor nations and non-governmental organizations were doing their best to prop up the newly-elected, democratic government and provide for the basic health and food needs of the people. In most respects, it was an uphill battle with Sisyphus leading the charge. Bureaucratic inefficiency and endemic corruption within the Liberian government conspired to keep the boulder from making much progress. The country's viability and very future were in serious question. Otherwise, things were just hunky-dory.

Jersey Briggs, my former colleague and erstwhile friend, had convinced me to come out of retirement and take the assignment. It didn't take much convincing since I was bored and broke. His offer gave me the opportunity to overcome both desultory conditions. I readily agreed before hearing the details and considering the dangers involved in accepting the job. I could be especially impetuous when money was involved. Patriotism came in a distant second but still served as a plausible excuse for my desperate, dissolute and pecuniary desires.

Jersey was the Director of Investigations for the U.S. Department of State, Diplomatic Security Service; the same position I held until I retired some years ago. We've had an on-again, off-again relationship for years. That meant I didn't fully trust the fucking bastard! He had suckered me into dangerous situations before and had no compunctions about doing so again. Hiring me was a no-lose situation for him. If I succeeded in solving a tough case, he'd garner most of the kudos. If I failed, he would tell his superiors that old Avery had lost his touch and should be removed from the reserve rolls for future assignments; put out to pasture like a broken-down dray horse. In any case, DS would effectively distance itself from any political pratfalls by not assigning an active duty agent, just a retread who had obviously outlived his usefulness to the outfit.

Sometimes loyalty and camaraderie were also in short supply among those who protect and serve.

My notional assignment was to conduct an in-depth review of DS's antiterrorism assistance program in Liberia. It was a suitable cover under the circumstances and one that would hold up under scrutiny by the local security services, the U.S. embassy and the DS advisory team providing assistance to the Liberian Special Security Service. I only prayed my beard stayed intact long enough to get the job done so I could get the hell out of here. If it didn't stay put, I risked much more than losing face.

The Special Security Service was the Liberian government organization charged with protecting the president, senior officials designated by the president and visiting foreign dignitaries. Its mandate largely mirrored that of the U.S. Secret Service but that was where the comparison ended. The SSS or Triple S, as commonly called, had been used by previous regimes as an instrument of terror and repression, largely a goon squad that reputedly had murdered, raped and kidnapped opponents and ordinary citizens alike without concern or consequence.

During its history, some of its agents had been characterized as sadists who engaged in gruesome acts of torture and cannibalism during the country's darkest hours. Some of these men, the worst of the worst, were assigned to the SSS Special Antiterrorism Unit. Now the entire organization was being restructured, equipped and trained by the U.S. government—all in the name of fighting international terrorism.

An important change occurred with a democratically elected president in 2006—Ellen Johnson-Sirleaf. She was the first woman elected to such high office in Africa and represented a bright ray of hope for the people of the Godforsaken country. One of her first acts was to request personal protection from the U.S. government. She didn't trust the Triple S since many of its senior leaders opposed her candidacy and reportedly were involved in thwarting her election to office. She'd also been hunted down by the SSS during the war years and had never forgiven them for that little episode in her life that almost caused her execution at its hands.

Moreover, there was the issue of the Triple S reputation in Liberia. She needed time to purge the organization of those members she considered undesirable or disloyal. President Sirleaf had even gone so far as to recommend changing the organization's name to the Executive Protection Service to remove the stigma that still haunted the peoples' minds and memories. That and other positive changes affecting the SSS were pending passage in the Liberian congress. She was one bound-and-determined lady who had publically vowed to professionalize the SSS, even if it killed her. The fellow members of her Unity Party constantly worried about the same outcome.

President Sirleaf had initially requested the U.S. Secret Service to provide agents for her security detail. The Service turned down the request noting it was outside the scope of its duties and authorities.

She next asked the State Department to send Diplomatic Security Service agents to provide similar protection.

The department declined but offered to fund a modest-sized security detail comprised of American contractor personnel for a limited period of time for her personal protection—just enough time for her to purge the senior leadership of the Triple S. The department also agreed to field an antiterrorism assistance team to Liberia to mentor and advise the reconstituted Triple S in achieving an acceptable level of professionalism and proficiency. The team would work in Liberia until the Triple S reached that magic level of competency or antiterrorism funds dried up or a new U.S. administration decided otherwise. The protection team had departed many months ago, but the advisors might be on the ground for years to come. Respect for basic human rights could be a difficult concept to accept for an organization that for many years had a freehand and sometimes itchy trigger finger.

The undesirables in the organization were quickly replaced by the president's trusted friends. Unfortunately, personal loyalty sometimes took precedence over experience. That had serious repercussions regarding the Triple S achieving a level of viability consistent with the advisors' mission, U.S. government objectives and the president's own desire. A five person team, comprised of retired DS special agents, now tried its best to coach, cajole, mentor, monitor and help transform the organization into a professional security service. The going was tough and progress was measured in tentative baby steps rather than leaps and bounds.

Regardless, the one thing the advisors never ever did was to protect, or suggest that it protected, the president or anyone else in Liberia. There was simply too much potential political fallout to assert such a claim. So, the Americans were merely advisors and nothing more. The Triple S maintained sole responsibility for the president's safety and most certainly not the U.S. government. It was an important distinction for political correctness and PR spin alone. God forbid something should happen to her on America's watch!

While the advisors roles and responsibilities were clear, at least in their minds, the State Department and the administration's decision to field an advisory team and fund an antiterrorism program in Liberia was less so. That was because there wasn't any terrorism as defined by the U.S. government or serious threat of terrorism in the country. The threat from what were called *former combatants* was of some potential concern since most possessed combat experience and access to arms that hadn't been recovered by the government at the end of the fighting. However, the fear had not materialized although crime was another matter altogether. That was because former combatants had been responsible for much of the violent crime throughout the country. That distinctly antisocial disease remained the most pressing public safety issue of the day.

If there was no credible terrorist threat to Sirleaf or the government of Liberia, why would the U.S. government provide antiterrorism assistance? I wondered.

The answers I believed could be found in the unique and special relationship between Liberia and the United States. That and the fact that Liberia had just elected a democratic government headed by a very capable woman no less, a first for Africa. Perhaps there was another, less charitable motive too.

Liberia was founded by the abolitionist movement for freed American slaves in the early part of the 19th century. Many former slaves and freeborn blacks migrated to the country over the next century or so as part of the back-to-Africa movement. It didn't take long for the newcomers to subdue the indigenous tribes and dominate political life in the country. The Americo-Liberians as they were called had little in common with their backward, native brethren. Their social customs and cultural perspectives had been forged in the United States. As a result, many American icons and institutions were adopted by Liberia. For example, the U.S. dollar served as official currency and its flag closely resembled that of the

United States. It was the only foreign nation that had named its capital after a U.S. president—James Monroe. Even its executive, judicial and legislative branches of government were patterned after those in America.

Many other examples of Americanisms and Americana existed throughout its culture and institutions. The special bond between the two countries had not been broken for almost two hundred years. Perhaps it was because the slavish nature of the White Man's guilt tended to die hard in the lopsided relationship. Perhaps it was something altogether different nowadays.

Ellen Sirleaf had been educated and worked in the United States for many years and was a friend of President George W. Bush and Secretary of State Condoleezza Rice. Bush had visited Liberia twice during a two year period while in office, both short day trips. For a sitting president to visit a backwater, West African state was largely unprecedented. Visiting it twice was considered highly suspect by many of the pundits and politicos who tracked such things. *Eh, what's up Doc?*

Liberia held no geopolitical or other interest for America, except one—potentially huge, off-shore oil and gas fields that hadn't yet been tapped and exploited. These large reserves, now owned by former American slaves, offered temporary relief to energy hungry Americans. The exploration and mapping of the fields had been completed and preparations were underway to begin drilling. Coastal, West African countries from Nigeria to Angola had already sprouted offshore oil rigs. It was now Liberia's turn to cash-in on its natural resources in a big way. It was the country's sole hope for economic salvation. The avaricious players on both sides of the Atlantic were gushing about the bright prospects on the horizon.

The decision to aid the new Liberian president with her personal safety concerns was a laudable and predictable act. It was another example of democracy building in action and a shrewd business move that would likely result in more obscene profits for the big U.S. oil companies. The United States most definitely wanted

President Sirleaf to have a long and successful stay in office. So much so that it had already urged her to run for a second term. She would be seventy-two if that should happen. Her continued tenure was good for Liberia and good for America: a win-win situation for both countries. The Liberians desperately needed oil money to rebuild the country and the United States desperately needed the energy. Friendly, bilateral relations didn't get any more symbiotic or cynical than that—just business as usual and another foreign policy success. Chalk one up for the good guys!

Speaking of being bushed, I was dead tired from my flights and the six hour wait between the Brussels to Monrovia leg of the trip. My embassy driver dropped me at Sea Suites where the embassy leased several furnished apartments for temporary assignees like me. I was too exhausted to even unpack. Instead, I chain-smoked several cigarettes and listened to the rain pound on the corrugated metal roof of my apartment. The pummeling sounds, Mother Nature's soothing white noise, had a relaxing effect and I slept soundly for the next twelve hours.

Sometimes those who protect and serve were so wet behind the ears they didn't anticipate the dangers intimidating or inundating them in Liberia's dampest season.

CHAPTER 2

MUMBO JUMBO

My first appointment of the day was at the U.S. embassy located in the Mamba Point section of the city. The driver deftly avoided the numerous potholes, pedestrians and other vehicles we encountered along the route. The intervening fourteen years hadn't improved the road or living conditions and things were actually much worse than during my previous visit. And they certainly weren't great back then. The lengthy civil war had set the country's progress back at least a generation. Fortunately, there were no stop-lights to contend with because there was no municipal electricity. Like the chaotic, dizzying streets, Liberia was stuck in a seemingly bottomless vortex in which only the strongest and most aggressive would likely survive.

The entire passing scene was thoroughly depressing and seemingly hopeless. The government was overwhelmed by the severe economic and humanitarian situation and could only beg for help from outside sources. However, largesse only came in small packages these days. Countries in the region couldn't help much because they had economic problems of their own. So, the new president undertook missions to the capitals of the richer nations of the world to appeal for money and equipment needed to rebuild her nation. Washington, DC, Beijing, Berlin, Tripoli and London were favorite stops on the frequent itineraries abroad. Hat-in-hand diplomacy was now the order of the day. But getting the country back on its feet again would be extremely difficult and problematic at best. Truthfully, it needed a damn miracle or very rich uncle to survive. Maybe some oil to grease the wheels of progress would help too.

I wore my best leisure suit to the meeting—the crimson one with faux pearl buttons. My black wingtips were shined to a high gloss. I stored my pack of Marlboros and Bic lighter in my pants pocket so as not to create an unseemly bulge in my jacket. I wanted to appear presentable and professional to my colleagues. I thought I looked particularly spiffy as we said in certain, closeted circles. Perception and self-delusion, rather than substance, counted for a lot in the State Department.

Following the perfunctory security screening, I was promptly ushered into Jackson Smyth's office located on the ground floor of the chancery. I immediately shook hands with him and then turned to Phil Jensen who was sitting on a small sofa next to the window. Jackson was the embassy Regional Security Officer or Security Attaché. Like his counterparts around the world, he was a DS Special Agent who simply changed monikers while assigned abroad. The title was less important than the function—the U.S. government's top cop and security official for Liberia. Since he was many years my junior, I only had known Jackson by his corridor reputation in the department. It was a solid one.

Phil Jensen was another matter altogether. We'd been contemporaries in the Diplomatic Security Service, although never directly worked together during our careers. However, we had carpooled for a number of months from the Virginia suburbs to Main State and had gotten to know one another fairly well. He had a long and distinguished career with DS having served many years overseas as a Regional Security Officer in some of the world's hotter spots. By the way, that didn't refer to the localcs climatic conditions unless you counted the incendiary security and political situations in Lebanon and the Philippines during the tough times. Phil was retired but had returned to harness as a contractor serving as the senior security advisor overseeing the State Department's Anti-terrorism Assistance program for Liberia. That meant he was the number one guy on the proverbial hook and responsible for professionalizing the Triple S.

Phil had two masters to satisfy in that role: the DS Anti-Terrorism Assistance Office in Washington for general policy guidance and the embassy RSO for operational matters within the country. He had to walk a fine line between the two and keep both organizations informed and content. The balancing act wasn't always easy given the internecine battles that flared-up from time-to-time.

Sometimes those who protect and serve needed the presence of mind and a couple of ambidextrous alter-egos to cope with bureaucratic tugs-of-war and clownish juggling acts.

Phil Jensen spoke first. "Hi Avery and welcome to the bottom of the third world. Why would you volunteer to come to a shithole like this when you could be kicking-back in the real world with the drinks and the ladies? As I recall, you liked both very much and occasionally to excess."

Phil was well aware for my penchant for wine and meaningful, casual sex. I had earned a certain reputation over the years for those weaknesses, along with a few days of unpaid leave for some of my more outrageous indiscretions. Despite my flaws, I was also universally recognized by my peers for my work ethos and tenacity as an investigator. Those qualities had saved my tenuous career and skin on more than one occasion.

"Phil, dedication and patriotism would be my first explanation, not the fact that I'm flat broke and need the money. My few virtues and many vices are getting expensive these days, my friend.

Besides, I had nothing better to do and looked forward to escaping the Washington winter for awhile," I quipped.

"Also, I haven't seen you in about 15 years and thought it high-time to renew our acquaintanceship."

Both laughed at my silly answer. However, the money part was absolutely true. Nothing else I'd say today would be because I'd been sworn to secrecy by Jersey Briggs. Only the ambassador and President Sirleaf had been briefed on the true purpose of my visit to Liberia via a NODIS, eyes-only cable from Washington. I didn't care for the fact that I couldn't reveal my mission to trusted colleagues but Jersey was adamant that I maintained cover for as long as possible to avoid any inadvertent leaks. The consequences of premature disclosure of why I was here could be disastrous for the mission and me personally. Given his logic and my innate instinct for self-preservation, I didn't bother arguing the point.

"Avery, we received notice of your arrival from ATA and understand the purpose of your visit is to conduct a program review of the Liberian SSS operation in terms of our assistance. However, a two-person team was here less than 10 months ago and did the same thing. We came out smelling like roses. So what gives? Why's there another review so soon?" Jackson pointedly asked.

Jackson was sharp and asked the logical question. I was sharper though and had a bullshit, but wholly logical answer.

"The reason is the Hill. The oversight committees are breathing down the backs of all government agencies providing foreign assistance to make sure Uncle Sam's monies are being spent properly and judiciously—the old waste, fraud mismanagement stuff again. It's a direct result of the reported widespread abuses in Afghanistan and Iraq, not so much the nickel-and- dime programs like in Liberia and elsewhere that DS funds."

"It's a matter of the small fish getting caught up in Congress's big dragnet. Regardless, DS, with its relatively modest dollars to fund the programs around the world, is on the spot. We're required to provide a report to the Hill within 90 days on each of the programs along with a certification that each is in full compliance with set spending limits and that funds are being expended as authorized. There's no mystery here, just more bureaucratic rigmarole."

"But couldn't I have done the same thing and submitted a compliance report?" Jackson retorted.

"Sure, you could have, but how much credibility would it have if challenged by the Hill staffers? Jackson, you and Phil are part and parcel of the program here and not exactly unbiased observers. Look, I'm not, nor is DS, questioning your honesty or integrity. That's not what this is about. DS headquarters correctly concluded that both of you are much too close to the situation and that's why an outsider must conduct the review. It's certainly nothing personal. Similar reviews are scheduled for Afghanistan, Indonesia, Pakistan and elsewhere. Liberia's not being singled out for any special treatment," I blatantly lied through my smiling teeth.

"Okay, fair enough. I've been around long enough to realize that logic and reason don't often win the day in the department. Please give us a broad outline of what you plan to do and how we can help. Nothing personal Avery, but we have full plates here and can't afford to hold hands for our visitors, even DS colleagues," Jackson commented.

The last thing I wanted was Jackson's or the embassy's help. Despite local customs, I also didn't want to hold hands with him. However, my foot was now firmly in the door but I hoped no one would abruptly slam it on me. I didn't want to injure my reputation as a flatfoot in good standing. On-the-job injuries could sometimes be fatal in my profession.

"I anticipate working with Phil and his crew for the next few weeks. Phil, I promise not to step on your toes or get in your way. I appreciate your position because I've been on your end of the stick many times over the years. To get started, I'll need some background briefings and introductions. I'll also need a car and driver to get me around. I sure as hell won't drive here. By the way, where can I buy cigarettes and a good bottle of wine? We all have our priorities and particular vices, don't we?"

I didn't get or expect an answer. I certainly didn't bother to ask about the women because I never had any difficulty locating that commodity before. However, that last line got a little chuckle from both of them. I couldn't tell if it was a knowing chuckle or one that suggested I couldn't find such staples in Monrovia.

Sometimes those who protect and serve spoke in forked tongues that were tied tightly in many knots.

"Avery, this is a good time as any to give you the big picture story of the Triple S," Phil announced.

"Its story is closely intertwined with the political history of Liberia since the ouster of the last democratically elected president, William Tolbert, in 1980. That's a good starting point for perspective and context and one of the reasons why we're assisting the Triple S today."

"It's a bloody story of coups, countercoups, plots and counterplots, bizarre juju rituals, high-level corruptions, acts of terror against the citizenry, the grossest human rights violations imaginable, personal and tribal enmities and vendettas, sociopathic and sycophantic actors of various stripes and much more. It is a tale that speaks to the disintegration of a country and society that was founded on American principles and values. Avery, please sit back for your primer on Liberian politics and subsequent civil wars that brought this country to its very knees."

I waited for the popcorn to be served, but before Phil could begin his spiel, I asked for a brief intermission to go to the John and smoke a couple of cigarettes. I had gotten to know the embassy's John fairly well from my previous visit in 1992. Fortunately, he hadn't moved in the interim and I renewed his acquaintance in the nick of time.

I suspected Phil's telling could take awhile and I wanted to satisfy my bodily needs first. I didn't want to miss a word of what he was about to say. It sounded like the storyline would make for a good B-movie except the script was all true. However, the trailers of coming attractions were stalled in preproduction. I prayed for the sake of the country there wouldn't be any sequels.

"William Tolbert was the last democratically elected president before the country abruptly slipped into insanity, later to be followed by chaos, war and anarchy," Phil began. "Successive regimes led by warlords or their surrogate puppets ruled or tried to rule the nation. I say *rule* because *govern* is a much too charitable word to apply to the situation. Truthfully, rank, raw and brutal dictatorship is a much better descriptor."

"Tolbert was ousted in a military coup in 1980 by Master Sgt. Samuel K. Doe backed by our Uncle Sam. Doe's rule was characterized by corruption and brutality. More of the same was in store for Liberia in the coming years. A rebellion, led by Charles Taylor, a former Doe aide and leader of the National Patriotic Front of Liberia, began in December 1989. The following year, Doe was assassinated by another rebel leader named Prince Johnson whose forces had temporarily taken the capital."

"According to popular lore, the trussed Doe was taken before Johnson and forced to kneel in front of him. Johnson was sitting on the veranda of a home located on Bushrod Island sipping a cold Budweiser. Johnson repeatedly asked Doe where the government ledgers where located—the country's bank accounts. Doe refused to tell him or didn't know. Regardless, the encounter's outcome was predictable. On orders, one of Johnson's goons put a single bullet into the back of Doe's head. As he did, Johnson reportedly quipped 'this one's for you, bud!' It turned out that the sergeant had received the ultimate in corporal punishment, all accomplished in traditional, African style."

Both Jackson and I gave a little snicker to Phil's puns and wordplay. He had a reputation for his offbeat, politically incorrect brand of humor.

"During the mess, the Economic Community of West African States negotiated with the government and the rebel factions and attempted to restore order, but the civil war raged on. By April 1996, factional fighting by the country's warlords had destroyed any last vestige of normalcy and civil society. After much back and forth, the civil war finally ended in 1997. Some would argue there were *wars* because of intermittent periods of peace and calm—mox nix to me."

"In what was considered by international observers to be a free election, Charles Taylor won 75% of the presidential vote in July 1997. The country had next to no health care system and the capital was without electricity and running water. Taylor had also supported Sierra Leone's brutal Revolutionary United Front in the hopes of toppling his neighbor's government in exchange for diamonds that would enrich his personal coffers. It was always about getting money in any way, shape or form with all of these characters."

"Keep in mind that all of the warlords in this drama funded their operations through the mining and export of the so-called *blood diamonds* and extorting monies from the few international companies operating in Liberia at the time—the rubber plantations, timber producers and iron ore mines."

"But the sale of blood diamonds provided the bulk of money needed to finance and support their personal wars. The diamonds were mined in alluvial streams located in the mineral rich interiors of both Liberia and Sierra Leone. Men, women and children were forced to sift and dig by hand for these ruthless entrepreneurs. The laborers worked under the worst conditions imaginable from sunup to sunset, seven days a week in shallow, open pits. Many died from malnutrition, exhaustion, disease and sometimes lead poisoning from their guards' rifles. The diamonds were smuggled out of the country and sold or traded for munitions on the world's markets. It was an extremely lucrative trade and one that kept the various rebellions robustly endowed, almost indefinitely."

"Here's another point to remember. These wars were not ideologically or geopolitically motivated in the slightest. The foreign powers may have preferred one warlord or another for the sake of stability and peace but there was no meaningful financial or other support, overt or otherwise, to the warlords by the outsiders. The blood diamonds bought what was needed to further perfect and sustain the genocidal wars."

"In 2002, rebels—Liberians United for Reconciliation and Democracy—intensified their attacks on Taylor's government. By June 2003, LURD and other rebel groups controlled two-thirds of the country. Finally, on August 11, Taylor stepped down and went into exile in Nigeria. Gyude Bryant, a businessman seen as a coalition builder, was selected by the various factions as the new president. By the time he was exiled, Taylor had bankrupted his own country siphoning off $100 million. According to the *New York Times,* Taylor left Liberia the world's poorest nation. In 2004, international donors promised more than $500 million in aid to shore up the country's ailing economy. With many of these nations, the checks are still in the mail."

"In a November 2005 presidential runoff election, Ellen Johnson-Sirleaf, a Harvard-educated economist who had worked at the World Bank, defeated George Weah, a former world class soccer star. In January 2006, Sirleaf became Africa's first female president."

"In 2006, former president Taylor, in exile in Nigeria, was arrested and turned over to the International Court in The Hague to face trial on charges of crimes against humanity for supporting rebel troops in Sierra Leone's and Liberia's brutal civil wars that claimed the lives of about 300,000 people in the 1990s. Taylor initially refused to appear in court when his trial opened in June 2007. However, he subsequently changed his mind and the trial has now resumed. Don't look for a speedy verdict because his list of crimes is very long."

I was already well aware of this last bit of information but said nothing because I was bound to secrecy by the bureaucrats in Washington.

"Avery, here's one, important take-away message from all of this bloody nonsense—not a single rebel leader had the slightest interest in Liberia except what the country could provide each in terms of lining their own pockets. Forget the patriotic, nationalist, liberation, democracy crap they spouted to justify their actions. It was all eyewash to cover their true motive for taking power—money, money and more money. Unbridled greed was the only personal agenda for seizing control of the country and running it into the ground."

"The consequences for Liberia are now clearly evident. It has the highest unemployment rate of any African country, perhaps in the world. An estimated two-thirds of the people are said to suffer from posttraumatic stress from the fighting and deprivations. Critical infrastructure such as rail, electrical, telephone, water and roads has been destroyed or severely degraded. Basic health care is extremely limited or nonexistent; there are only 200 doctors to serve 3.4 million citizens. The people are still greatly suffering from the perverse, self-serving form of patriotism practiced by the rebel warlords."

"Let me transition to the Special Security Service at this point in my monologue. You'll hear many stories about the political situation and rebel wars while you're here so if I missed any high spots you'll be able to fill in the blanks. Everyone has a tale to tell because everyone in the country personally and poignantly suffered one way or another during the past fourteen years or so—and still continue to suffer. So much so that the government has convened a Truth and Reconciliation Commission that is slowly disclosing the traumas, abuses and corruptions of the war years. By the way, its hearings are broadcast live on the one TV station and over the radio. They're a very popular source of information and macabre form of entertainment here.'

"The Triple S has had a checkered past to put things mildly and diplomatically. It was originally established in February 1966 to provide protection to the president, vice president, other high ranking government officials and visiting foreign dignitaries—much like the U.S. Secret Service. By the way, that's still its sole role today under President Sirleaf."

"However, its reputation was so badly damaged during the Taylor regime that the current president has submitted legislation to change the organization's name. The atrocities, or crimes against humanity as the United Nation call them, that were committed by the SSS under Taylor were simply too obscene and offensive to the Liberian people to let the old name stand. Sirleaf wants change and professionalism and that's why we're here. It's a struggle to say the least but the U.S. is committed to giving it a shot. God only knows what will happen after we leave. Old ways die hard, especially in Liberia where violent, premature death has been a way of life for the past many years. I'll relate only the organization's history under Taylor since it's critical to understanding what is facing us in mentoring and advising the SSS of today."

"Charles Taylor was a military dictator and bully of the worst stripe. He was elected to office as the country's president in 1997, a cruel joke perpetrated on the Liberians by themselves. One of his first acts was to take control of the SSS and fill its ranks with his loyalists and cronies. Personal safety and survival were great motivators for him in those days. Most members of the service were former fighters in his NPFL rebel group, although many were simply thugs and sociopaths of the first order. The new Palace Guard was molded in his image and shaped to carry out his will."

"One could not resign from the organization for any reason because that suggested disloyalty and disloyalty suggested being summarily executed. One never wanted to be terminated for cause for any reason. Plots and paranoia ruled the organization's activities in those days. The dictator had to be protected at all costs because if he fell from power his underlings would too. Falling from power meant fleeing the country or imprisonment or execution by the next regime. These things were the only options for those officials who actively supported Taylor and his abusive, corrosive rule of the country between 1997 and 2003."

"However, Taylor's SSS also operated outside the palace gates with impunity as a paramilitary unit. The number of agents and operatives swelled to about 1,500 at its height and served as Taylor's personal instrument of terror that was most often directed against his own people, but later as fighters against the LURD rebel forces that vowed to topple his regime."

"In rural areas, particularly in remote parts of Lofa and Gbarpolu counties, armed SSS agents illegally entered homes, most often to steal food, money or other property. Members of the security forces in those areas generally were paid and provisioned inadequately and often extorted money and goods from citizens. Local communities were compelled to provide food, shelter and labor for members of the forces stationed in their villages. Human Rights Watch reported that President Taylor's SSS was also mobilized to combat LURD rebels. Again, the SSS then largely consisted of his former

NPFL combatants who were paid a one-time fee of $150 and were expected to pillage for food and other basic needs thereafter."

"I'll spare you the gruesome details of SSS activities—there are too many emotionally wrenching, despicable acts to relate. No doubt you'll hear many of them during your stay. They are so horrendous that I suggest you listen to them only on a strong, empty stomach after a couple glasses of wine—white Zinfandel as I remember from our earlier days in DS."

"Suffice it to say that Taylor and some of his senior cronies are undergoing trial at the moment in The Hague's International Court of Criminal Justice for crimes committed against humanity. Others are wanted and on the run. Others will escape justice altogether, I suspect."

Phil didn't realize it but he had just touched on the reason I was here—my true mission to Liberia.

"Avery, that's a quick and very dirty history of the Liberian political situation during the past couple of decades. It's not been a pretty picture and the country's current snapshot is blurred and sketchy at best despite the recent election of the Iron Lady of Africa, Ellen Sirleaf."

Sometimes those who protect and serve kept a straight face beneath an African mask to better conceal their nervous facial expressions and true intentions.

CHAPTER 3

PRAETORIAN GUARDIANS

My digs at the Sea Suite compound were pretty plush by local standards and much better than the converted shipping container I lived in for three months while conducting a major fraud investigation for the department in Afghanistan a few years ago. I hoped the accommodations were a favorable indication of things to come. Maybe my mission to Liberia would be a cakewalk after all as Jersey Briggs had suggested. Sure, maybe I would win one of the mega lotteries in the States or finally get to shack-up with Helga and Olga, the nubile Swedish contortionists I often fantasized about. Yeah, right, sure thing Avery. Keep on dreaming my friend if it comforts you.

More to the point, maybe I should have had my head examined before accepting the damn assignment! I was now terribly worried about what I was up against and how I might gracefully exit from this little drama with my head held high or at least still atop my shoulders. I know, I know, heavy is the head that wears the crown.

However, my neck was so bowed at the moment that I couldn't help but notice that my black wingtips needed a shine.

It had rained again throughout the night. I awakened several times by what I first thought were the sounds of gunshots very close by. I reflexively took defensive action by pulling my sheet over my head and praying that it was only a neighbor being attacked. As young agents-in-training, we had practiced this tried-and-true defensive technique over-and-over again as a security blanket and comforter in times of danger. It worked and I quickly fell back to sleep.

In the morning, I identified the attackers—pear-sized almond fruits that had fallen from the trees onto the metal roof above my bed. By the large number of shell casings lying on the ground, the act was an obvious gangbang by a bunch of out-of-control nuts. Okay, one case solved but another big one to go before I'd sleep soundly again.

Sometimes wishful thinking, misguided altruism and old-fashioned self-preservation motivated those who protect and serve.

Phil Jensen had offered to take me on a short tour of the key sites associated with SSS protective responsibilities. It didn't take long to hook-up with him because he only lived two doors away from me at Sea Suites. Our first stop was about three miles down Tubman road, the same one that fronted the Sea Suites compound.

"Welcome to my world, Avery," Phil greeted me with a grin as we got into his Nissan Patrol SUV and headed to President Sirleaf's residence.

"This has been my home away from home for the past eighteen months. I have about four more to go until the current contract ends. I don't know or care if it will be extended. In any event, that will be it for me. I'm pretty well burned-out at this point and looking forward to rejoining my family back in Virginia. Enough is enough! I've paid my professional dues and then some since I've been here."

While chatting, Phil carefully negotiated the many road obstacles in our path—open manholes, ruts and bumps hidden by standing water, school kids darting in-and-out of traffic and the numerous walkers who used the macadam roadway for travel rather than the water-soaked, dirt shoulders. But worst of all were the small, yellow taxis, invariably Nissan Sunnys', that would abruptly stop in the middle of the road or cut in front at the last second to snag a fare. The fact that many didn't have working taillights and turn signals made the experience all the more challenging. I sat more upright in my seat and tightened my seatbelt a notch but Phil didn't blink an eye at all of the happenings before us. I suspected for him it was just another, routine commute to the office.

"We'll be arriving at the president's compound in a couple more minutes," Phil casually mentioned as he avoided a pothole large enough to swallow the front axle of our vehicle.

"It's time for a shift change and you'll get to see the SSS presidential security detail in action. Her Nibs is leaving this morning for the airport for a flight to New York to attend the annual United Nations General Assembly meeting. Maybe we'll tag along and check on how they handle the motorcade. We routinely do this as part of mentoring and critiquing performance."

"Phil, remember those days when as young agents we actually looked forward to the event. It was nonstop work and partying for two weeks each year. It was a great opportunity to reconnect with colleagues from the various field offices and headquarters. I also recall it was a great opportunity to get hammered and laid. Those were fantastic times."

"Those were the days my friend, I thought they'd never end……" I sung in my husky, smoker's voice. That little bit of singsong garnered a loud groan from Phil. I knew then I hadn't lost my touch for bringing joy into other people's lives.

"Jesus Christ! What the hell is going on?" Phil exclaimed as we pulled through the entrance to the president's residence. Before us was the motorcade with all of the vehicles lined-up and positioned as taught. Obviously, interpersonal relations and anger management techniques were not being taught because about 30 or more SSS agents and drivers were shouting and jostling each other. It appeared that the Midnight Shift going off duty and the Day Shift coming to work were engaged in a heated argument.

"Stay in the car Avery and observe. I'm sure this little dustup will be grist for your program critique and a black eye for me and the advisors. God, talk about bad karma and timing! The president is scheduled to depart any minute," Phil muttered as he slammed the door and ran to the commotion.

I didn't envy Phil's situation. He and his team didn't supervise or manage the Triple S. The only thing he could do under the circumstances was to referee the situation as best possible. I wished I could tell him he didn't have to worry about the incident as far as I was concerned. There would be no program review or report. That wasn't why I was here.

I watched as one group of agents, presumably assigned to one shift, tried to physically remove the agents sitting inside the vehicles. I guessed those agents comprised the other shift, but I wasn't sure. No one had thrown a punch or drawn a weapon but the situation was tense and might easily spin out of control.

Phil was now speaking to someone who appeared to be a senior SSS officer. I would later confirm my hunch. He was Frank Yeaten, the SSS Deputy Director for Operations, who was in command of the security details for all officials and dignitaries protected by the organization. Others soon joined them in discussion; likely the shift leaders.

After about 15 minutes or so, the situation dramatically calmed. The agents occupying all of the motorcade vehicles got out and allowed their colleagues to take charge. The departing agents and drivers didn't look happy but it seemed they had now complied with whatever decision and order was made by their superiors. It looked like a mini crisis in discipline among the ranks had narrowly been averted at the 11th hour. Actually, it was 8:30 when the president departed for the airport. She didn't have a clue as to what had just transpired and wouldn't learn of the incident until well after her return to Liberia.

Phil was fuming, red in the face and highly agitated when he returned to the vehicle. I didn't ask him what had happened. He would tell me in his good time and way when he cooled down. He had known me well enough over the years and knew he could confide in me. I would never betray his confidence or trust. I bided my time and bit my tongue while we drove to the Ministry of Foreign Affairs—the temporary home to the Office of the President, the SSS and the American advisors. Phil was so pissed-off that he didn't bother to shadow the president's motorcade to the airport.

We parked in front of the MFA but Phil left the vehicle running to keep the air conditioning going. It was only about 9:00 am but the combination of heat and humidity was already oppressive. It was raining lightly and I didn't mind waiting for a few minutes to let it stop. I couldn't get used to carrying an umbrella and had forgotten mine at the apartment. Old age, I guessed. No matter, I was much too crusty to melt.

"Avery, you just got a good taste of what we're up against here," Phil finally spoke as he idly stared out the windshield.

"It was simply another example of the undisciplined, immature nature of the SSS—weak senior leadership and little self-discipline in the lower ranks. Effective and sustainable command and control measures within the organization are largely nonexistent or disregarded. Personal agendas, political affiliations, old friendships or vendettas, and tribal allegiances are much more important things in their society. Perhaps up to two-thirds of the force has no sense of duty or responsibility, except to themselves."

"What you just witnessed was an argument over money—*small money* as it's called here. President Sirleaf customarily hands out packets of money to the people that see her off on international trips. She's done this since she took office and now everyone who wishes her farewell expects a handout or *white envelope* as they refer to it. In this case, the Midnight Shift insisted on accompanying her to the airport even though the shift had just ended. They refused to turn over the vehicles and weapons to the Day Shift. I found out that even one of the security vehicles was hidden at an adjoining compound so the oncoming shift couldn't find it. It planned to join the motorcade on the road to the airport."

"Okay, money was on the table and both groups were jockeying for a piece of it. Is that basically it?"

"Yep, it is, but there's some history here. This is not the first time this has happened and it's symptomatic of the lack of professionalism on the part of the SSS as a viable security service. Can you imagine what would have happened if the Iron Lady had walked into that mess? She would have been furious and rightly so. I can assure you she would have fired everyone present, including me."

"But here's the real issue. How do you instill a fundamental sense of duty and personal accountability into a people that have lived in fear, repression and economic hardship for the past generation? Now, with a true democracy, the average Liberian believes he or she has almost unlimited personal rights but they have no sense of the responsibilities that go along with them. I'm convinced it's a direct response to the tyranny they have lived under for the past many years. Prior to 1980, most people lived in a democratic society where there was a sense of nationalism, unity, and a collective will to live in peace and harmony. No more, my friend. Everyone's now out for themselves in making a buck any way they can and regardless of consequence. It's really a sad comment on today's Liberia."

"I understand that self-interest was of paramount concern in order for people to survive in the war years. Order and discipline during those bad times were achieved by intimidation, bribery or the barrel of a gun. Whatever worked, worked back then."

"Unfortunately, those are not options for us as advisors. We have to cajole, coerce, convince, prod, connive and sometimes capitulate to get the most basic things accomplished in terms of equipping, training and mentoring these guys."

"Remember Avery that we're still associated with a diplomatic security service and we have to act accordingly," Phil mentioned while smiling. Actually, it was more of a grimace.

Minding one's P's & Q's was often more important than making progress for those who sometimes protect and serve.

"There are numerous examples of significant SSS screw-ups and ineptitudes that I can cite. In retrospect, many would be hilarious if they weren't so damn serious. All of these things add-up to a big question mark as regards the Triple S's ability to protect the president of Liberia. And make no mistake, she takes her personal safety very seriously, as she well should. She's made many enemies over the years in her quest to bring stability and democracy to the country. In doing so, she's thwarted the financial and political aspirations of those who would like to return to the corrupt, personally profitable, good old days."

"Phil, I'm curious, how much money will each of the motorcade agents and drivers likely receive?"

"About five, six bucks a head. They earn two hundred a month so I suspect that it's big money to them. Regardless, they're paid well by local standards. Come on, let's get a cup of coffee and I'll show you more of my little kingdom from Hell."

So far, so good, I thought. I had successfully conned Phil and Jackson as to the purpose of my visit to Liberia. My cover story didn't have to hold-up long though. I understood it was perishable and that was okay. I just needed some time to put my plan in place and see what happened. Both would soon learn why I was here and they would be royally pissed that they hadn't been cut-in to the operation at the beginning. However, that was impossible now given the constraints I was working under.

I simply couldn't afford to show my hand just yet. The

consequences of premature disclosure or exposure would likely damage its outcome and my longevity. That wouldn't please me one bit. I still wanted to collect my Social Security allotment to supplement my federal pension that had been halved by divorce.

But, most importantly, I had now insinuated myself into the bowels of the SSS. I was searching for one of its major turds and was now positioned in the perfect place to do so. If I had my way, he would be flushed out soon and pay for his unspeakable crimes against humanity. I'd make sure to respectfully raise the toilet seat in his honor after I finished with him.

Sometimes those who protect and serve were often motivated by a mix of patriotic, professional and peculiar desires—and scatological allusions.

"Avery, we're located in the MFA because the government's Executive Mansion experienced a suspicious fire about a year ago that totally gutted it. It sits empty because there's no money to rehab it. That's the way things work here," Phil mentioned as we entered the foreign ministry's only operable lift.

That was strange—they called elevators lifts in Liberia, I mused. I always thought those were the things I used in my shoes to give me more stature. I always wanted to walk tall and proud as an American should. But maybe I needed to replace my wingtips with a pair of cowboy boots for a heightened perspective. Regardless, Liberian English and customs were often difficult to comprehend as I would soon learn.

"The Office of the President and SSS occupy offices on the fifth and sixth floors. We've got a small office adjacent to the president's," Phil commented, opening its door.

"Guys, I'd like you to meet Avery Dick who's here to conduct yet another inane review of our performance," Phil quipped as we entered the office. "He's not so bad for a Washington prick and retread like the rest of us."

I was quickly introduced to George Lamont, Bill Hammond and

Dan Bricknell, all retired DS agents now working under contract as security advisors. I learned that the last member of the team, Jerry Burton, was on home leave in the States. These were the folks who tried their best to professionalize a mismanaged, fractious and dysfunctional organization comprised of about 425 people.

Sure, just whip them into shape from scratch in a few months for your Uncle Sam, boys, I aimlessly thought. *But make damn sure you do it while walking on eggshells so you don't ruffle any political feathers. By the way, be careful not to foul your own nest while you're doing it.*

"Coffee, Avery?" Dan politely asked. I later learned that Dan was Phil's butt-boy and gopher, much to the dismay of the others. I suspected that Phil rather enjoyed the subservient relationship. Voluntary servitude seemed to be in vogue for those willing to denigrate and demean their selves. Regardless, servile eunuchs, active duty or retired, were still highly prized commodities in any organizational setting.

I declined the offer because I was anxious to start my investigation, but not my program review. I didn't waste any time getting to the bottom of the bottom line.

"I've already briefed Phil on the purpose of my visit and he can fill you in on the details later if you don't mind." I began.

"I need to be hooked-up with a car, driver and handgun. I was told in Washington those things wouldn't be a problem."

"I'll give you the name of a rental place and have the SSS provide a driver to get you around," Phil replied. "I'll also get them to issue you a SSS identification card. That little item will give you authority to rape, pillage and plunder—also to carry a weapon and make arrests of anyone in the country without concern or probable cause. The authority's a carryover from the old days when the SSS was a power unto itself. Only the president of Liberia could overrule its decisions and actions. Again, that's been an issue we've had to contend with here—aligning its protective roles and responsibilities with internationally recognized standards of conduct. That's President Sirleaf's strong desire and a big part of our mission."

"As to the handgun, we can give you a Glock 17 and a couple of magazines for your personal safety. By the way, are you still reading *Soldier of Fortune* and *Hustler*? Do you need a holster or plan to stick it down the front of your pants, as usual? Avery, be careful or you might accidentally shoot off your surname," he chuckled.

"Speaking of accidental discharges, please don't shoot yourself in the foot on my watch as you reputedly do from time to time. That's too much damn paperwork for me to handle and the medical care really sucks in Liberia."

"Oh, thanks buddy," I sarcastically responded. "I sincerely appreciate all the help and camaraderie, my old, geezer friend—and I do mean *old*!" That retort brought a few small laughs from the equally small audience. I suspected Phil ran a very tight ship in terms of managing his staff and didn't tolerate challenges to his authority. However, I may have just made a good impression with his subordinates with my little inanity.

Sometimes those who protect and serve didn't always respect their elders or betters in the often less than diplomatic Diplomatic Security Service.

CHAPTER 4

MERCY! BEAUCOUP

"Good morning, Mr. Poppy. Okay, you are welcomed to Liberia, my friend."

However, that wasn't quite what my driver had just spoken in Liberian English, only a rough approximation. I had trouble understanding what he actually said since syllables were contracted or dropped outright in the spoken language. Moreover, words were adopted or adapted that made no sense whatsoever to outsiders. I had picked up on some of the lingo during my previous visit but I was still confounded by most of what was said in ordinary conversation. The locals would sometimes add a lilting "Oh" to the end of a phrase or sentence. It had no particular significance in a grammatical sense, just an exclamation and more gibberish to confuse the non-Liberians, I believed. If that was the intent, it worked very well indeed!

Regardless, Moses Kekula had just warmly and respectfully greeted me in his nation's semiofficial language. I suspected I would understand more of the patois later. We shook hands ending with the customary, West African finger-snap. I could never get the hang of it but always tried just to be polite. Regardless, it was never a snap for me.

Sometimes those who protect and serve didn't have the ear for foreign languages, patience for native tongues or any digital dexterity.

Given his last name, Moses was a native son of Liberia, not a transplanted Americo-Liberian whose predecessors had immigrated to the country in the 1800s. Johnson, Jones, Brown and Taylor were clearly names derived from their former masters in the United States. Kekula was a name from one of the country's many indigenous tribes. It had likely been transliterated from a phonetic pronunciation in Kru, Mandingo or Vai or one of the other 20 tribal languages.

The significantly smaller number of immigrants had subdued the tribes many generations ago through bloody warfare. Cannon power turned out to be the great equalizer when it came to leveling the playing field. Liberian fodder was plentiful in those days.

Moses had more that 30 years service with the Triple S and had survived many purges during his tenure because he was merely a low-level driver who had a knack for avoiding serious accidents over the years. He was also very servile, someone who opened car doors and ran personal errands for the senior managers. His defensive driving skills, demeanor and utility to his masters had spared him from premature termination of both his employment and life.

He had seen much during his time and might serve as an excellent source of information. He had many stories to tell, I suspected.

My first stop was the SSS warehouse that housed all of the organization's personnel records. I'd been given carte blanche to look at the files by telling Phil I wanted to review the results of the SSS recruiting and vetting process. I wanted to verify that background checks were being conducted on applicants and to confirm the documentation was complete and sufficient. Of course, this was all a big fib but a necessary one for me to access the one file I was searching for. I worryingly checked my nose for any suspicious signs of unwanted growth.

I spent the next hour or so poring over personnel files that I randomly selected from the HR file cabinets. I did this to establish credibility with the clerk who watched over me. I asked questions about the hiring process and jotted down notes to sustain the ruse. As hoped, he soon became bored and wandered off. Through him, I had learned which cabinet contained the files of former employees.

I now had the raw, paper files in my grasp of everyone who had worked for the organization since its inception in 1966. The simple plunger-lock was easy to bypass and open with a bent paperclip. It took me about ten minutes to locate the folder I was looking for because the records weren't maintained in any order, alphabetically or otherwise. The clerk simply didn't follow prescribed rules for proper filing. Evidently, he hadn't learned his *ABC's* or lesson on trusting nosey foreigners.

Merci Beaucoup's personal history folder was now in my hands. If my plan worked, his hands would soon be cuffed and legs shackled as he was spirited out of the country to The Hague to stand trial for his horrendous crimes against humanity. This human monster was my quarry, my nemesis and my recurring nightmare. In any case, he was a dangerous character and I wouldn't foolishly take him for granted. Rather, I would track him down and bring him before the bar of justice, dead or alive. Of course, I meant him.

Sometimes those who protect and serve had sticky fingers capable of withstanding the traumas of nasty paper cuts.

Thanks to Merci's mother an abomination was born in Lofa County located along the French speaking Guinean border on June 3, 1969. She must have had a warped sense of humor to name him after an expression of civility and cordiality. She died in childbirth and wouldn't know the monster she had delivered into the world on that fateful day. Regardless, many Liberians would come to understand the sick irony and curse his name much later—Merci Beaucoup, mammy!

Merci was born with albinism, the genetic aberration that afflicted perhaps one out of a hundred thousand people. Moreover, he was cursed or blessed by total albinism or amelanosis where the hair, skin and eyes were fully white due to the lack of melanin pigment. Unlike other African cultures, the Liberians considered Merci a novelty and a sign of good fortune from heaven. In his case, they got their directions mixed up—he was the Devil's spawn sent directly from Hell to torment his countrymen.

Torturing small animals and sometimes other children of his village was just child's play for the unrepentant sociopath that he was soon becoming. Young adulthood would bring him more trophies and perverse gratifications as a rebel fighter for Charles Taylor during the war. Killing, raping and mutilating people for sheer pleasure became the hallmarks of his military career and subsequent tenure as the director of the Special Security Service. Charles Taylor loved him like an older brother. Time and circumstance would reveal that the two shared much in common.

Booku became his transliterated name but he was later nicknamed *No Eyes* because he always wore dark-lens, wraparound sunglasses. Common folklore claimed that he didn't have eyeballs, only empty sockets lined with diamond chips. The tiny mirrors gave him great powers to see all things clearly. The same juju allowed him to move with ease day or night with unfailing sight—a white zombie with a shaved skull who was always clothed in black from head to foot, including a black beret atop his head. He also wore a large, inverted gold cross hung on a silver chain around his neck to complete his macabre, Halloween costume.

He dressed for dramatic effect and the effect terrorized everyone who came into contact with him. The lore also suggested that if he ever removed his sunglasses and stared into someone's eyes, the viewer would die a horrible death at his hand. He was Death personified and incarnate too. In other words, he was one over-the-top badass, scary and crazy dude! The persona suited him well for what he had in mind for Liberia.

Sometimes poor dressing skills and megalomania had to be overlooked and ignored by those who protect and serve.

Moses Kekula had been patiently waiting for me outside the records repository. He didn't bother keeping the car running. He had long ago become accustomed to the unrelenting heat and humidity—and to the working environment in the SSS. He graciously opened my door and I stepped into the interior's furnace. It was stifling hot and I ordered Moses to turn the AC up to full-blast. I also instructed him to turn on the air as soon as he spotted me heading for the car. I couldn't stand the heat even though there was no kitchen to get out of at the moment.

Moses chuckled at my discomfort and had probably witnessed similar reactions with similar visitors many times over during his long career. I suspected pain and discomfort were familiar aspects of life in Liberia. One either learned to cope with the situation or leave the country. While leaving was a desirable option for many people, only very few could afford to do so. The remainder toughed-out life as best they could under the harsh conditions of climate and calamity.

"Where to my new boss man?" Moses inquired. I wanted to say any place cool but held my tongue. I was profusely sweating and not in a particularly good mood.

"Sightseeing," I eventually replied. "I want to see all the tourist attractions Monrovia has to offer."

That sarcastic line got another, bemused chuckle from him. Actually, I was interested in reorienting myself to the city and observing ordinary street activities. Local color didn't get much darker than here. It was depressing blackness and gloom virtually everywhere I looked.

"Anyplace in particular?" he asked.

"No, I just want to see the changes since I was here in 1992."

This time Moses didn't chuckle. He must have seriously misplaced his earlier sense of humor.

Apparently, funny bones were in short supply like everything else in the country, even the Humerus ones. That was because offhanded, and often disarming, jokes, were regularly exchanged between the rebels and government forces during the bloody civil war. Persistent hunger led many combatants to discover that certain parts were totally tasteless. Regardless, numerous amputees could now be seen pleading for handouts on the crowded street corners of Monrovia—so much for cutting-edge, black humor these days.

My little slice of reverie was preempted by someone moseying back into my higher consciousness.

"That's a long time and much has occurred since your last visit but none of it good, my friend. We're much worse off now than 15 years ago. It's hard to believe but Liberia was once a relatively prosperous, stable country. We had many international flights into and out of Roberts International in those days. We had a thriving fishing industry and municipal electricity was available in most cities in the country. Roads were built and maintained, food was plentiful and affordable, health services were very good and people got along well. It was a good life, one worth living."

"But no more, I'm afraid those times are gone forever. No one is particularly interested in rebuilding our country. Foreign governments, especially the Chinese and Americans, are funding reconstruction projects of one kind or another, but the average Liberian could care less. That's because we're a traumatized, beaten people who have no hope for the future. Today's Liberia is all about looking after one's self first and foremost, making money and surviving long enough to spend it. The quick, easy buck is the new God for the people. Listen to casual conversations and you'll find that money is the number one topic. The subject dominates our thoughts and actions. It's sad but true, we don't believe in anything else these days. We don't dream anymore."

I sat back and absorbed what Moses had just related. If what he mentioned was true, the Liberian people were living in a fugue state—that was neither a red nor blue one, just dark black with little hope for a brighter hue anytime soon. That might explain why Merci Beaucoup was reportedly so successful in recruiting people for his insidious cause. He was both a feared and revered figure among much of the rural populace where Charles Taylor still had wide support. Merci was someone who could rally recruits around a common goal that held appeal for many Liberians who felt disillusioned and disenfranchised over the current regime and regimen.

The lofty aims of President Sirleaf and her Unity Party were alien to those who favored a strongman to lead the country out of the chaos. They were people who were geographically and politically distant from the seat of government in Monrovia and didn't share the president's vision for a modern, prosperous country based on democratic ideals and principles. To them, dictatorship was a predictable, effective and preferable form of home rule. The pervasive government corruption, violent crime and deteriorating economic conditions could only be turned about through strong leadership backed by the barrel of an AK-47 rifle and the unwavering will to use it to solve the nation's many problems.

To many, Merci Beaucoup was the right man for the job. His very peculiar, patriot zeal and unfettered ruthlessness had been tested and affirmed many times during the country's civil wars. Not surprisingly, he didn't disagree with his supporters' views of his qualifications and fitness for leadership. He had been planning a return to power for many years and was taking his role as the next president of Liberia very seriously by galvanizing the former followers of Charles Taylor to his cause.

My French was a little rusty but *coup d'état* were the words I was searching for in the back of my mind. I wondered why the act of overthrowing a democratically elected government sounded much less threatening and frightening when spoken in a foreign language.

Sometimes those who protect and serve preferred to safely and discreetly parse their written words in a wholly frivolous, passé lingua franca.

As I pondered, Moses pointed. We had just driven through the central business district and were now heading across the bridge to Bushrod Island. He pointed out the collapsed bridge that ran directly parallel to ours and commented that the Chinese had agreed to rebuild it. That would be a sign of progress but the people were still skeptical that it would ever be rebuilt. As we passed the Port of Monrovia, Moses mentioned it was one of the largest ports on the coast of West Africa, but in poor repair. More progress was still needed, he joked.

Shops of all description lined both sides of the four lane road that led out of the city. People were also hawking their wares on the median and at the sides of road. This activity presented another level of difficulty in terms of driving in Monrovia although Moses took all the action in stride and continued on without dropping his speed.

Honestly, most of the buildings looked like they belonged in an inner city slum. However, this location was an important commercial hub and source of imported goods. Sellers and buyers alike haggled over price amid the passing traffic. No one seemed upset in the slightest by the activity or the close calls with injury or death.

We ended our abbreviated but informative sightseeing trip at the Monrovia Brewery, home of Club beer, on the outskirts of the city. Suburbia didn't quite describe the locale. Moses suggested a tour of the brewery, but I declined. I had to get back to my apartment to prepare for an important meeting set for early in the evening. Unfortunately, Moses had just missed out on a couple of free beers. Crying in them was likely a national pastime.

"Just about a mile further on this road is the St. Paul River. It was an important dividing line that separated Monrovia from

Greater Monrovia during the wars," he spoke while negotiating traffic.

"What's Greater Monrovia?" I asked

"Monrovia was on this side of the river controlled by the government forces. Greater Monrovia was on the other side controlled by the rebels—the rest of the country. It was our little joke at the time. The other dividing line is located on the other side of the city, just past the Coca Cola bottling plant on the road past Paynesville," he added for good measure and equanimity of beverages.

As we returned on the same road, he asked if I knew what Liberians called the mode of transportation of the people walking on the sides of the road. I didn't and he couldn't wait to tell me.

"They're travelling by Mandingo bush taxi!" he exclaimed while laughing. "It's a popular way of getting around these days since most people have little money to pay for a taxi or bus ride."

I suspected he had used the line many times over with equally gullible visitors. How he could maintain a sense of humor under these conditions was beyond me. I was already depressed about what I saw and heard. I needed a drink, a couple actually—soonest!

Sometimes those who protect and serve found that *Happy Hour* was not always funny.

CHAPTER 5

GOLDEN FLEECING

7PM was our meeting time and the Golden Beach Bar and Restaurant was our appointed place. The American security advisors called the restaurant the *Golden Fleece* because of the high prices—at least high by local standards. It was a popular spot for expats and the few Liberians who could afford the prices. It was also a popular spot for the many hookers looking to score with those who could afford their prices. The food was a mix of local dishes and Western fare. The local dishes typically sat at the large semicircular bar and hoped to be selected from the ersatz menu as a takeaway dessert. I only wondered if everything was equally safe and edible at the establishment.

I had arrived early to take in the scene and to detect any indication of surveillance. I hadn't noticed anyone or anything suspicious but it was virtually impossible to be certain. Regardless, business was good tonight but I was able to snag a table in one of the thatched cabanas on the beach. It would give us some privacy and concealment. What we had to discuss was of critical importance to our mission and Liberia. Our personal safety was at risk too and we had to be damn careful going forward. We would both have to rely on tried-and-true tradecraft to see us through what would be a tough, almost impossible task. The stakes were high and we had to succeed. Otherwise, one very troubled, potentially oil-rich nation and American ally would soon be headed by the most ruthless and vicious dictator imaginable—all thanks to a Mr. Merci Beaucoup.

I ordered a glass of white Zin, sat back and smoked a couple of cigarettes while waiting for my guest. However, *guest* was not an accurate word to characterize my soon-to-be relationship with her. Confidante, coconspirator, colleague and trusted partner were much better descriptors. We would need to rely on each other to succeed and survive. Backs needed to be protected as well. Simply put, our lives were in each other's hands. Such relationships didn't get any closer or more intimate in this business.

Mary Tambo was many things at once: a dual national with American and Liberian citizenship; a former refugee who had lived for many years in the United States with her parents during the Diaspora; a member of the Bassa tribe, an honors graduate in international relations from Smith College, a staffer with the United Nations Mission in Liberia—and an undercover operative of the U.S. Defense Intelligence Agency. Most importantly, she would be my partner.

According to her personnel folder, Mary was a trusted operative whose loyalty to the United States was beyond question—the polygraph didn't lie. Moreover, from her photograph on file, she was a very bright young woman. In her case, *bright* meant light skinned. *High-yellow* would have been the term used several generations ago for women of such hue. It seemed that one or more white bwanas had gotten into her ancestors loincloths at some point in her lineage. Regardless, she was a very attractive woman who also happened to be extremely intelligent.

Just as I was reflecting on my partner-to-be, a voice from behind me asked: "Avery, is that a Zinfandel or ordinary blush? I can't tell the difference given the similarity in color."

"It's a fine, White Zinfandel," I gushed and blushed. I was

thoroughly embarrassed that I'd missed her approach. I wondered why because my hindsight had always been 20-20 before.

"Good, order one for me. I think it's important that we get to know each other's tastes and vices," she laughingly said.

"It will take you awhile to learn all of my vices, my virtues much less so. Care for a cigarette?" I asked as we shook hands.

"No thanks, I don't smoke, other than the occasional joint. Please don't mention that little disclosure during my next update investigation. The Washington bureaucrats don't seem to have much tolerance or humor when it comes to such things. However, they don't seem to care if one commits slow suicide with tobacco or alcohol, but God forbid if someone gets a nice high from weed. It doesn't make any logical sense to me. But hey, I just work here."

I immediately took a liking to Mary. She had a rebellious streak in her that appealed to my quirky side. She was also quick on the uptake and had a good sense of humor. Her pretty face and lithe body added to her other likeable attributes. I was entirely taken with her personality and presence. Okay, so much for the bullshit platitudes. I thought she was one very hot bitch!

"Avery, where do we start? There's so much to discuss and do."

"Let's begin with what Booku is up to in the bush. You've been following his activities for the past six months or so and probably know more about him and his plans than anyone else in the country. Let's start with his fleeing Liberia in 2004."

"I'm not so sure about the *knowing* part because his intentions and movements are difficult to track and predict, but I'll tell you what I do know and what I speculate. I'll try to keep them straight so we don't confuse the two. That could be disastrous in terms of developing a plan of action to bring him to justice—either the American or Liberian kind. As you already know, he's a despicable monster that doesn't deserve to live. Pardon my vehemence, but he was personally responsible for the deaths of several of my relatives and untold others during his miserable, bloody existence on this planet."

"Merci Beaucoup, Jesus, what an ironic name for a sociopathic sadist! Yes, he fled the country right after Charles Taylor did the same. His power base was gone and he rightly feared for his life if he stayed. Rumors have it that he initially fled to Sierra Leone and then to Togo where he reportedly served as an officer in the Togolese army. There were only very sketchy reports as to his activities and whereabouts until he was first spotted in Lofa County, Liberia about a year ago."

"Historically, Lofa was his homeland and source of protection and support. It was, and is, Taylor country where many people wish for the return of the former president to power. Beaucoup was a top lieutenant of Taylor's and a commanding figure in his own right. With Taylor standing trial in The Hague, his many supporters have now switched allegiance to Beaucoup. It doesn't seem to make any difference to them which one rules the country as long as it's a strongman and favored son who'll share the spoils of office with his loyal brethren."

"Avery, you have to understand some things about what's going on in this country for context and perspective. First, President Ellen Johnson Sirleaf's fighting an uphill battle to restore democracy and reform and rebuild the nation. While she was initially a very popular candidate for office, she is at the two year mark in her tenure. People are getting impatient waiting for her to fulfill her many campaign promises for a better life."

"One of her first acts was a plea to all Liberians living outside the country to return home and participate in rebuilding the nation. She promised a better life for those who answered the call. Many did return but the situation isn't any better; in many respects it's much worse. The shortage of consumer goods coupled with inflation is one persistent problem. Rice is the main food staple for the people. The price of a 20 kilo bag of white rice has jumped almost

40 percent in the past three months alone. The salaries of the few Liberians who hold jobs have not kept pace. The increase in the cost of rice and other consumables is largely blamed on rampant government corruption and therefore the Sirleaf regime. Huge supplies of rice are donated by various nations and international relief organizations but much is diverted and sold on the black market. The people are well aware of this fact as they buy sacks of the grain with markings clearly indicating they've been donated by USAID or the Peoples Republic of China or whoever."

"There's another issue that is perhaps more pervasive and insidious, but difficult to pin down in terms of Sirleaf's popularity. She and the majority of her Unity Party are Americo-Liberians. However, the vast majority of the populace is made up of indigenous tribesmen. The historical tensions and frictions of the past two centuries remain between the two factions. As you're probably aware, the Americo-Liberians have been dominant in the country, holding many of the better paying jobs and key positions in government and commerce. So there's resentment by the have-nots that plays into the equation."

The waiter interrupted Mary's spiel by asking if we were ready to order. We were. Mary ordered the traditional, popular Liberian/West African dishes of Fu-Fu, pepper soup and, of course, rice. I had spaghetti with Marinara sauce and a side of garlic bread. I also asked for another glass of wine to wash it down.

Admittedly, I couldn't stand the local food since I'd witnessed the preparation of these culinary delights during my previous visit. That act alone turned me off from eating them. Fu-Fu was made from the cassava root that was placed in a small cloth sack or large sock and beaten into pulp. The juices would leech out through the cloth leaving the end product the consistency of coarse mashed potatoes.

The only variation on the theme was the gravy or sauce poured over the concoction. It could be about anything and usually was. Sweet and/or sour gravies were desirable toppings. Pepper soup consisted of a beef or chicken broth to which spicy peppers were added for desired effect. Sometimes pig's feet, dog meat or other offal were included in the recipe for additional nutrition or comic relief. I was never certain which and I didn't care to know. Regardless, the stuff was God awful!

Mary and I quietly ate our meals and she resumed telling her story of Merci Beaucoup and Liberian politics. I couldn't stomach watching Mary eat her meal and stared out at the ocean the whole time. My spaghetti was actually very tasty, the wine even better.

Sometimes those who protect and serve had to be exceedingly polite in the presence of quasi-foreigners who had no appreciation or respect for fine American cuisine.

"Where was I? That's right, the Americo-Liberian controversy. Ever since the Sirleaf administration took power in 2006, there's been public apprehension over the high number of government officials who reportedly hold dual Liberian, American citizenship. There've been heated arguments over the role of Liberian exiles who were repatriated to work for the Sirleaf-led regime. During the election of President Obama, many dual nationals were reported to have voted by absentee ballot. Most Liberians see this as evidence of a much too cozy relationship with America, especially given the prospects for huge oil revenues."

"Moreover, there is strong resentment felt by those who stayed during the war years against those who fled the country. Those who fled are considered by many to be cowards and unpatriotic. So, now you have some idea of what President Sirleaf is up against in governing this fragile, fractious country. These obstacles don't even include the threat from Merci Beaucoup. He's the number one concern for the president in my opinion. He must be stopped at all costs before he can bring Sirleaf's government down. If Sirleaf falls from power, America's oil supply from Liberia will cease. Avery, it's as straightforward and simple as that—no Sirleaf, no oil."

"Mary, that's all very interesting but we need to get back on point. Our objective is to capture or thwart Booku and, by doing so, stop his plans to destabilize and overthrow the Sirleaf government. The government corruption, the Americo-Liberian tensions, the purported nepotism and cronyism, the broken campaign promises and the privations and hardships being experienced by the people are matters internal to Liberia and outside the scope of our assignment. It's really none of our business. Besides, we can't deal with those things in any case. Our marching orders are narrowly defined and specific—get Merci Beaucoup and hope our efforts keep Sirleaf in power for a few more years so the United States can exploit the oil reserves sitting off the country's coast. Tough American love and real politick in action, I would say."

"I understand the American position but you need to understand the realities in Liberia that impact our actions and decisions. They're interrelated to a large extent and need to be considered before going forward, as I would say. We can agree to disagree, Avery, but we need a unified approach and a solid plan of action regarding Booku. Agreed?"

"No argument here, let's hear the rest of your intelligence collection efforts. What's the man up to now in your opinion?"

"As I mentioned, Booku has been seen a number of times in the past few months in Liberia, mostly in Lofa County. Given the number of different sources, I believe this information is true. He's also been spotted in different villages located in the Eastern half of the country—Taylor strongholds. He appears to be laying the groundwork for recruiting combatants and establishing several training camps. My nominal boss, the Defense Attaché at the U.S. embassy, has ordered overheads of these areas and it looks like swaths of jungle have been cleared and structures resembling barracks being erected as we speak. I've checked and discovered the Liberian government is not involved in such construction. Also, there're no private sector activities in these remote areas as well. So, our tentative conclusion is that Booku is building training facilities for his soon-to-be army."

"There's something else that may fit into the building of training camps—weapons caches. For years, there have been rumors that Booku had collected and buried arms in the jungle for safekeeping and future use. The rumors are well known and continue to be passed along to this day. They have become *rural legends*, if I can use that countrified expression.

These legends say that after Taylor took power, thousands of weapons were recovered from his former combatants. The weapons—AK-47, rocket-propelled grenade launchers and other munitions—were placed into 55 gallon metal drums and buried in locations only known to Booku and his boss. He did this under direct orders from Charles Taylor. The lore holds that the drums were securely sealed with lianas that had been soaked in a tar solution. When they were pliable, the cords would be fitted to the rim of the drums and the lids attached. The woody vines would eventually dry and contract, forming a tight, waterproof seal that protected the contents. Once the drums were placed into the holes, those who dug them would be shot and buried as well. Booku wanted no one but himself and Charles Taylor to know where the goodies were hidden. Two sets of maps were allegedly prepared; one for Taylor and one for himself. Neither map has been located, if they actually exist."

"I have no clue whether the legend has any credibility but I don't discount it as simply a folktale without some plausibility. That's because the Liberian government has publically admitted that tens of thousands of weapons were unaccounted for and missing when the fighting finally ended."

"Avery, there's one more thing. Admittedly, it's a bit sketchy and vague but I'm following it nonetheless. Merci Beaucoup may be insinuating some of his followers into Monrovia and other large cities where his support is weak. Generally speaking, Sirleaf has her strongest support and political base in the cities where the population is better educated and somewhat better off financially. The numerous government jobs that are doled out keep both her loyalists and critics alike employed and relatively prosperous or at least fairly content for the time being."

"I've had one report that suggests that Booku is sending his people to the cities and ordering them to join the local Community Action Groups that operate in virtually every sub-district. The CAGs, as they're called, are civic organizations that primarily serve as vigilantes because the law enforcement forces are so weak and ineffectual. Violent crime is probably the number one concern today for the average person. The police are so inept, corrupt and indifferent the people take justice into their own hands. Keep in mind Avery that the Liberian National Police were only rearmed in the last few months and then only special groups called the Emergency Response Units. *Unit*s is a bit of a misnomer in this instance since only 150 or so officers have been deployed to date—all in Monrovia. The country has three and a half million people—you do the math."

"What's intriguing about this possibility is the fact that Charles Taylor used the same ploy as a rebel leader knocking on Monrovia's door in the 1990s. He dispatched trusted soldiers to infiltrate the CAGs, thus creating a sizeable, fifth column of loyalists. They reportedly were engaged in disinformation campaigns that included the killing of international peacekeepers and leaving articles of clothing implicating the government forces. It was an effective, diabolical strategy that further confused and frightened the people. Maybe that's what we're beginning to see here. Time and further intelligence reporting will tell."

"What I don't understand is why President Sirleaf doesn't send the Liberian army to the Eastern counties to nip this thing in the bud. She's got to be fully aware of what's unfolding before her eyes. Why doesn't she act," I forcefully asked.

Mary laughed at my question. "*She can't* is the short answer."

"The AFL, the Armed Forces of Liberia, isn't capable of putting up a decent fight. Like the National Police, it's still ill-equipped and trained to take on Beaucoup. The logistics alone would make such a venture foolhardy and reckless. The Liberian National Army is presently incapable of sustained action against an adversary that has wide support in remote regions of the country. Its overly stretched supply lines could easily be interdicted and destroyed with little difficulty. It also doesn't have the expertise to wage war as a newly-formed, green organization. Lastly, I don't believe the army has the will to fight. It was disbanded after the civil wars and is only now being reconstituted and trained by the Americans. It's simply not ready to engage anyone at this point."

"By the way, the issuance of weapons is a highly charged issue given the country's history of violence. The United Nations has unfettered control over how and when those weapons will be employed. Given the UN's past performance around the world, I wouldn't expect it to approve any action by the Liberian army that would rock the political boat."

"What about the United Nations taking on Merci and his soldiers on behalf of the government of Liberia? It must have some sense as to what is going on and can see the possible results of doing nothing," I asserted, getting more frustrated by the second.

"The United Nations Mission in Liberia's mandate is to maintain the status quo at all costs. It mentors and advises the Liberian government on all matters of administration and governance but little more. Its peacekeeping role is limited to observing and reporting any civil disorder. It doesn't take sides in what it views as merely internal matters of a political nature. Look, few UN troops assigned here have any real combat experience. Most have been trained in logistics, supply, civil affairs and administration. That's virtually all they do in Liberia."

"The vehicle checkpoints with armed UN soldiers you see on some of the roads are eyewash. Not one of the foreign contingents would lay down lives for the sake of Liberia or the Sirleaf regime. The Nigerians, in particular, have served off-and-on in Liberia for many years. They've witnessed a succession of wars and dictators who had no interest in the country whatsoever—other than to pad their offshore bank accounts. Do you really believe that any of them would put themselves on the line for a dysfunctional nation that has little or no interest in helping itself? I don't think so. What's your guess?"

I'd had enough of Mary's dismal account of the political realities in Liberia. I was ready for bed and told her so. She didn't take me up on my indirect proposal for sex so I decided to call it a night. I didn't bother to order dessert, either the confectionary or carryout variety. Neither appeared that appetizing or appealing. We agreed to meet again soon since we still needed to come up with a strategy, a game plan, course of action or a wholly plausible excuse for failing in our mission.

Sometimes those who protect and serve could be terribly intimated by a bright, beautiful woman with brains but no discerning taste in food or men.

CHAPTER 6

HONESTLY DISINGENUOUS

"For Lord's sake, Phil, this ain't frigging Hawaii!" I shot back in response to his previous statement. "50? Are you serious?"

"Completely," he replied to my little outburst of incredulity. "Actually, the numbers run from 50 to 54 for the SSS. 50 is the number assigned to the director. The others are designators for his four deputies."

"The Liberian civil service system long ago assigned numbers to identify senior positions in the executive branch. The practice of referring to officials by their numbers still exists in most government departments and agencies today. It's simply custom and a sign of respect."

"So when I'm introduced to the director, should I call him *fifty* or *5-0,* Dan-O?" I facetiously asked for numerical correctness. I didn't know why I was so surprised with the fact that numbers were used because DS often did things by the number. In its case, the Hawaiian good luck sign—number one—was the most common digit flashed between colleagues in passing.

"*I am pleased to meet you director Heller* would be a good opening line. Thankfully, you're not meeting Sirleaf so *Your Excellency* and *Madam President* are not on the table. Avery, I don't why you're so uptight over a simple courtesy call on the director. Both of us have done this bit of diplomatic shtick many times over during our careers and with much more high-profile dignitaries."

"Yeah, I remember meeting a few queens when I conducted background checks in New York for DS, but I still don't like the experience," I quipped while taking a deep drag on my Marlboro.

Sometimes those who protect and serve detested protocol pretentiousness as well as forced genuflection.

Walter Heller was an Americo-Liberian who appeared to be in his mid-sixties. He was a stalwart Sirleaf supporter and trusted confidant. That's why he was appointed to the job in the first place. Nothing else, such as experience, counted for much these days. Like many Liberians, he had sought refuge in the United States during the bad times in the country. This fact caused some resentment among the SSS rank-and-file agents that had toughed-it-out by staying—the ones who didn't have enough money or influence to flee.

I introduced myself and shook Walter's hand. I managed to produce a wimpy end-snap; his sounded like the sharp crack of a whip. I'd never get the hang of this little West African practice. Fortunately, he wasn't wearing a ring so I could dispense with that little bit of protocol ritualism. However, I adamantly refused to honor his Seiko in the same manner. After all, I did have to watch out for my timeless, limited and sketchy self-esteem.

"Welcome to Liberia Mr. Dick, I hope you enjoy your visit. As you already know, we're experiencing difficult times and appreciate the help from our American friends. By the way, Phil speaks very highly of your long experience."

"Thank you director, it's a pleasure to be here again," I forced myself to reply.

Fibbing in such circumstances was a learned and valued trait in the Foreign Service. It filled in the blanks in otherwise bland, largely senseless diplomatic discourse. I had gotten fairly fluent in the lingo over the course of my career where fibbing was expected and customary, but outright lying wasn't—unless you avoided getting caught. Regardless, plausible denial and spin counted for everything in this game of frangible wordplay—scout's honor!

"I've explained to Avery where we're at in terms of assisting the Triple S," Phil spoke up. "The firearms and other equipment have been procured and distributed, the new SSS headquarters building is almost ready for occupancy and most of the formal training has been accomplished, although there are a couple more training courses coming up in the next few months. I expect at that point the USG will scale back our personnel and role. Our mission will largely be completed by then. I'd guess that President Sirleaf will have to petition the department and White House for us to continue maintaining a presence here. As we all know, she's a very persuasive lady and may convince the powers to let us stay longer, perhaps to the end of her term in office. We'll see."

"Phil, I can confirm that the president would like the American advisors to stay as long as possible," the director replied. "It's not only the training and equipping of the SSS that concerns her. She is worried about her personal safety and the presence of Americans close by gives her a sense of security. While we've made great progress in getting rid of the bad boys in the SSS, there's still the possibility of some rotten apples in our barrel."

"We're constantly looking over our shoulder and have an internal security unit that operates to identify any possible threats to her safety from within the organization. Someone on her security detail could assassinate her given his or her close proximity. It would be easy. That act could precipitate the overthrow of her administration and plunge the country into chaos. From the chaos, a strong dictator could emerge to rule our nation, just like in the past. That's why we're so sensitive about this possibility. It's not only Sirleaf's life that's at stake, but our fledgling democracy that's also at great risk. We aren't being paranoid, just extremely cautious because the political environment we work in is murky at best. We must always be on guard against the insinuation of her sworn enemies into our camp. Violent coups are part of our country's troubled past and we don't want any future ones. Liberia can ill afford more turmoil and bloodshed. We've had too much of both."

I actually empathized with the guy and his predicament. Protecting the Iron Lady of Africa carried an awesome responsibility.

"You have a tough job director and I don't envy your position in the slightest. You have an almost impossible situation to contend with. I wish you and your nation the best of luck. More to the point, I don't plan to make it any more difficult. As I explained to Phil and the embassy's regional security officer, I'm here at the direction of the department to conduct a review of our government's antiterrorism assistance program for Liberia. My role is straightforward; just check the books to make sure U.S. government funds have been properly expended. I don't anticipate any problems knowing that Phil's an unrelenting taskmaster when it comes to passing the buck," I joked to break the gloomy talk of assassinations and coups.

Phil rolled his eyes at the pun but the director quickly shot back a response to my feeble attempt at levity.

"I can assure you that all monies and equipment received from your government have been judiciously spent and can be accounted for down to the last Liberian dollar, Mr. Dick. We would never buck the system or underhandedly bite the hand that feeds us, as you might say," he laughingly quipped.

The director had a good sense of humor and enjoyed the punning. He needed every bit of joviality he could muster given his situation and the state of the country.

We exchanged pleasantries before concluding the meeting. I promised to brief the director on my findings before I left the country. He might be in for some surprises. Then again, I might be too if I weren't damn careful or downright unlucky.

Sometimes those who protect and serve mumbled goodbyes with their tall tales tightly tucked between their legs.

"That wasn't so bad was it, Avery? Other than your inane pun about passing the buck, I mean. But what the director didn't mention is interesting and that bit of trivia might give you a better sense of how the Triple S is seen here as an institution—its old baggage, so to speak. The baggage isn't very pretty, but it was fashionable for awhile. However, I suspect that Louis Vuitton would've cringed at the sight and left town with luggage in hand," Phil lamely tried to pun. *But in his case, it suited him,* I mentally countered.

Phil and I were heading back to his office and I was about to get another primer on the SSS by the sounds of it. I badly needed a cigarette but didn't want to interrupt his storytelling. I could tough it out though—both listening to his story and awaiting my nicotine fix. *Ok Phil, let's get this over,* I anxiously thought. Ironically, I would soon learn that coffin nails were the only plentiful items in Liberia during the Taylor days.

"As you already know, a ghoul named Merci Beaucoup was the SSS director under Taylor. He's a merciless sociopath who's now on the run for committing crimes against humanity. During his four-year tenure, he was personally responsible for the gruesome murders of Taylor's opponents, real or otherwise. His reputation for ruthlessness was known to every man, woman and child in this country. I suspect many people still suffer nightmares when they hear his name."

"Mr. Beaucoup's over-the-top ego and warped sense of humor knew few bounds. As director, he drove a black Toyota Land Cruiser with heavily tinted windows. The vehicle's license tag read SSS-50. People would flee when he drove the streets of Monrovia, especially at night when most of his extracurricular duties were carried out. People called it the *hearse* or *meat wagon.* If someone was invited or forced inside, it was a one-way, downhill ride for the victim. He or she simply disappeared and never to be heard from again. One certainly didn't want to hitchhike when the vehicle roamed the streets. Even the rank-and-file SSS staffers were terrified when they received an after-hours phone call from the director telling them to come into the office. Of course, he would be pleased to send his car to collect them from home."

"On occasion, victims would reappear, certainly not alive but to serve as reminders of Beaucoup's power and his determination to hang-on to it at all costs. At his order, SSS goons manning the security checkpoints into the city would erect ersatz drop lines using the intestines of their victims. The guts would be strung across the road and raised or lowered to allow traffic to pass or halt. Typically, the victim's head would be stuck atop a nearby pole and prominently displayed for all to see. It served as a gruesome reminder that the SSS was an all-powerful force to be reckoned with."

"The same goons would also gamble to pass the time. In one game, they would bet on the gender of a pregnant woman's unborn child. Typically, two goons held the woman down while another slit her womb with a cutlass while she was still alive. By the way, people use the word *cutlass* to describe any sharp-bladed weapon. I guess it sounds more swashbuckling and less threatening. These guys often laughed at their bloody handiwork. However, the little object lessons in cruelty and insanity worked well on the public's psyche. Nobody challenged the unbridled authority of Beaucoup or the SSS while Taylor was in command."

"Given its checkered past, President Sirleaf vowed to clean house and restructure the organization from top to bottom. She's accomplished much of that already. She brought Director Heller back from the States because he was a loyal, trusted member of her inner circle. He's no fool and realized that public perceptions of the SSS were almost as important as real change. One of his first acts was to permanently retire Mr. Beaucoups's Toyota and replace it with a white Nissan Patrol with the tag number SSS-1."

"Avery, Liberians aren't colorblind and likely would recognize the symbolism that might suggest positive change. Time will tell if it helps remove some of the organization's stigma and stigmata. Keep in mind that things aren't always black and white here so the jury's still out on this one, my friend."

Sometimes those who protect and serve often used offbeat and off-road vehicles to dissect gory, depraved acts of cruelty.

CHAPTER 7

SKETCHY SKULLDUGGERY

I had done my due-diligence diligently by laying down a heavy smokescreen concerning the real reason for my visit to Liberia. I just hoped that no ill winds would blow in my direction before I finished my dangerous assignment to the country that God had absentmindedly forgotten. Maybe my pack-a-day habit would help protect me or at least keep the mosquitoes at bay.

I think everyone had fully swallowed my bullshit cover story. I only worried about Phil who might harbor some doubts about why I was here. He hadn't challenged it but I had an uncomfortable suspicion that he questioned my bona fides and veracity. We had known each other for a long time and both of us had a sixth sense when it came to duplicity. That was due to our long careers in DS where dissembling behaviors were normal and expected roles for those who protected and served themselves. In any case, he had stayed mum so far. I only hoped he would keep it tightly affixed to his jacket lapel.

My rounds to spread the word of the second coming of Avery

Dick to Liberia had gone well. I actually received much more information on the local situation and the SSS than I gave. It was all useful stuff to my cause because I didn't arrive with that much skinny from Washington. But now that I had insinuated myself among the unwitting, it was time to take action against our foe, our adversary and worst nightmare, Mr. *No Eyes* Merci Beaucoup. I couldn't wait to see this out-of-sight character because this wasn't Gaza by any stretch of the imagination. No, this was blurry Liberia where everyone had to watch out for himself in order to survive.

"Ok Mary, how are we going to game this thing? My gaming skills are a little rusty because I haven't played in awhile. More importantly, you know the local scene and personalities and I don't. What're we going to do first?"

Mary Tambo and I were having dinner at the Mamba Point Hotel. DS tradecraft dictated varying our restaurants and menus for our overt, clandestine meets. Trying new cuisine came in a close second to our precautions. I recalled that personal safety measures must be practiced to perfection. In my case, I believed a medium-rare steak with a dollop of Hollandaise sauce was close to perfection. I'd stake my reputation on that assertion.

The flickering candles on our table accentuated Mary's good looks and sensuality. I noticed again what an attractive lady she was. However, I'd be careful not to gawk, at least not too much, while sitting across from her. Staring was okay but gawking was considered damn rude in my social circles. Drooling was out of the question. Of course, this was about how we spun and rationalized things in the Foreign Service. We just used interchangeable words to describe differences without distinctions. It all became routine, second nature after awhile for the seasoned, cynical professionals.

"Since we met a few days ago, I've been giving this a lot of thought. How do we stop Booku from overthrowing Sirleaf and sending this country back to a Hell on Earth? How do we thwart his plans for a violent coup and send him packing to The Hague to stand trial for his many crimes? How do we pull it off without getting killed in the process? How's your *Crème Brule* Avery?

"That's a lot of questions but few answers. By the way, the crème was fine," as I licked my spoon clean. But now it was time for Mary to get her own licks in and come clean. She did so without any prompting or spoon-feeding on my part.

"Here's what I think," she tentatively answered. "Booku is well entrenched in the far counties where he has public support and a sizeable following. I believe we should first concentrate on the immediate, proximate threats to the Sirleaf government. That would be the fifth columnists that I mentioned before. I've developed additional intelligence since we last met. My friends at the Liberian National Security Agency have passed along some interesting tidbits of information that they gleaned from phone records and cell call monitoring by some suspicious players in the Paynesville area that are especially worrying. It looks like the infiltration has started in earnest, I mean Paynesville," she quipped.

I chuckled at her little *bon mot*. It went well with my *Crème Brule*.

"Avery, Paynesville is what I would guess most of us would call a suburb of Monrovia. It's always been a largely lawless town and stronghold for Taylor sympathizers. It has a large, active Community Action Group given its high crime rate and lack of adequate police protection. The group is nominally a civic minded organization that promotes good works in Paynesville but in practice it's a bunch of vigilantes who police the town and administer their own brand of street justice. It's also very effective by most accounts and has popular support because of the ineffectual policing. Frankly, the police are afraid to enter Paynesville, especially at night, fearful for their own safety. Most cops in the country are not armed and risk being chopped or killed carrying out their duties to protect and serve."

"My sources tell me that two likely agents of Merci Beaucoup have taken up residence in one of Paynesville's neighborhood slums and have joined the Community Action Group as members in good standing. Both of these characters are from Lofa County and one has been identified as Amos Brown, a former crony of Booku's during his SSS tenure. Mr. Brown was also Booku's personal bodyguard in the bad old days. Avery, his hands are dirty too. He was responsible for the deaths and tortures of several Taylor opponents. He's one very bad actor who needs a good spanking. The other fellow hasn't been identified yet but my friends are working on it."

"It seems that the barbarians are now inside the gate. Mr. Booku is using the same tactic as his former boss to infiltrate Monrovia in preparation for a coup. Maybe what worked once will work again to divide and conquer Liberia. You can't argue with success, I guess. So the control of Paynesville has great strategic value in facilitating the introduction of rebel forces into Monrovia. Remember, the highway through Paynesville is one of only two gateways to the capital."

"The presence of these two guys represents an immediate threat to Sirleaf as I see it. Therefore, neutralizing them before they can spread disinformation and galvanize support to their cause should be our number one priority. What do you think? Avery"

After my third glass of wine I wasn't thinking too clearly, but I felt relaxed and mellow. Mary's information seemed solid and her suggestion was wholly logical. The two bad boys were our immediate concern. Clearly, we weren't ready to take on Booku in his own backyard yet.

"I think that's a smart move and good start. How do define *neutralize* in this instance?"

"Put the two goons on ice, take them out of play. Kidnap, I mean arrest, them and have the government authorities hold them incommunicado on trumped-up charges. Such things are done here and the law can be manipulated to make it happen, more-or-less legally. I'm sure the right Liberian officials would support this action given their great anxiety about a coup. Of course, they'd have to keep it quiet because the UNMIL weenies would scream bloody murder about human rights violations. What it doesn't understand or appreciate is the fact that the people have experienced human and civil rights abuses for the many years and much worse than what we're proposing. One more won't hurt if it can prevent another civil war or violent change in government. There's been too much senseless killing and we don't need any more."

"Okay, I agree with the plan but how do we go about making it happen. Neither a paunchy, middle-aged white guy nor a pretty, bright young woman fit the bill as plausible undercover operatives in this situation."

Mary laughed at my physical description of myself. It was wholly accurate but my feelings were hurt just the same. I ordered another glass of wine to assuage my emotional pain and enhance my mellow buzz. I lit another Marlboro while waiting for my drink and ego to recover its equilibrium.

"Let me handle the logistics of the op. I can get the people to work the undercover part to locate and grab these guys. Patriotism and money work wonders in Liberia these days. By the by, it costs about $50 to have someone killed here. Add another $50 and they'll throw in a nice church service and proper burial too."

I wondered how I would claim the upcoming expenses on my voucher. I couldn't say *bribe* or anything suggesting the facilitation of a crime, but I thought gratuity or stipend might work nicely for the bean counters back home. The word *stipend* had a particularly highbrow ring to it and could mean almost anything in government parlance. I firmly believed I'd have more buzzwords and idioms to claim before we rested on our laurels.

"Avery, I've done my part by coming up with our opening gambit. I think we can pull it off but I need some time to recruit the right people and set up a covert holding facility for the bad guys. But now it's your turn to use your gray matter and figure out the next steps to bring Booku down. Once he realizes his subordinates have gone missing, he'll be mightily pissed. He'll quickly conclude that the Sirleaf government is now aware of his scheme and he'll retaliate in some way."

"His supercharged ego will allow nothing less so we have to be prepared for some blowback. He still has some informants in the capital and they'll undoubtedly report anything on the street, no matter how seemingly insignificant. He knows Monrovia well and he'll use all resources available to find out who was behind the kidnapping of his underlings. We'll need to carefully watch our steps at that point. Good OPSEC practices will be the order of the day so we don't lose our way or lives. We'll need to be damn circumspect in terms of communicating and meeting with each other. But I'll really miss our alfresco dinners together."

I didn't know who Al Fresco was but maybe he was some sort of culinary guru or restaurateur in Liberia. I didn't want to show my ignorance so I didn't ask. Liberian English could be so damn confusing and intimidating at times. Hell, American English could be too!

"But we need to plan for follow-up actions against him. That's the tough part of the job. You need to come up with a strategy, a game plan soonest. Once we take his guys off the street, Booku will take-off the gloves and come after us. We need to keep him on the defensive as much as possible if we're going to succeed. Avery, come up with an offensive plan of action. Time's not on our side."

Mary was spot-on in her assessment of our situation. We didn't have much time once we moved against Booku. I would develop a course of action; come hell, high water or Merci Beaucoup. I was very adept at playing offensively.

Sometimes those who protect and serve were thoroughly confused and confounded by their improbable homework assignments.

CHAPTER 8

RUMBLE IN THE JUMBLE

I spent the next few days perfecting my cover story by poring over files and interviewing people who I had no interest in talking to. I also spent much time trying to come up with our next move to put Booku in his place—before the International Court of Justice at The Hague. If we had our way, he was going down to Hell's nether land to face trials and tribulations for his unspeakable crimes against humanity.

By now, I had fully co-opted Moses Kekula into our growing team of conspirators for a righteous cause. I only hoped our efforts ended with righteous effect as well. Moses readily agreed to join us out of a strong sense of Liberian-styled patriotism and a generous U.S. government stipend. I wasn't quite sure which one was the greater motivator. In any case, my expense report was steadily growing by the day. I was sure at some point I'd have to justify all of the costs to my masters. Given my experience with such things, I'd make sure the numbers added up correctly. Fraud was not condoned in the department. But memory loss was another matter altogether. It was a common affliction among those who protect and serve.

I instructed Moses to rent a nondescript vehicle for our extracurricular activities. It wouldn't have been good form to be seen driving around in an official Liberian government SUV, much less one assigned to the Triple S. I told him we needed to operate in mufti—he chose an older model Toyota Camry instead. It was a bit surprising since I hadn't explained the *difference without distinction* dictum to him yet. I was glad I didn't say *incognito*. We could have ended up in one of those ubiquitous yellow Sunny taxis.

Moses wasn't bright by any means but still very quick on the uptake. Regardless, he'd make an excellent U.S. citizen because he had few scruples and whatever principles he might hold could be easily compromised. However, his intestinal fortitude and moral fiber had yet to be tested and I didn't look forward to the experience. But that would surely come later when we least expected it. He seemed okay otherwise. So far, he'd kept me in one piece through his driving skills. Moreover, his stories about life's little ironies in Liberia kept me in stitches.

Sometimes those who protect and serve were savvy, foresighted judges of true characters.

Mary had been making good progress in her efforts to locate Amos Brown and his colleague in Paynesville. Actually, finding Amos was easy for her spies. He had such chutzpa that he was running for local office in the community. I guessed that *chutzpa* was Liberian for *big stones*. No matter, he was now a known quantity and relatively easy target for what we had in mind—a quick grab and run operation. Amos's colleague was less visible and we still didn't have a name to tag him with. No matter, Amos alone would be a rewarding, prized catch.

Our plan called for luring Amos to the SKD Stadium located on the outskirts of Paynesville. It was a large sports complex dedicated to former president Samuel K. Doe. It was also a perfect place for a snatch. Our hook was money. Through Mary's trusted agents, we had concocted a story that some friends of Booku wanted to contribute money to his coup campaign in return for a piece of the oil rights when he took power. It was a plausible bit of bullshit that Amos would still question. He would be suspicious but would still show up for the meet. The money was just too compelling to pass up.

If his boss learned that he had blown-off a chunk of money that could further his plans, Amos would be in big trouble. He was smart enough to realize that he had to go through the motions and test the waters. However, he didn't want to test the waters by being tied-up, gagged and thrown in the St. Paul River by Booku. Like most Liberians, he couldn't swim a lick.

We prepared for our nocturnal adventure by carefully rehearsing our roles. I also had Moses drive me to the SKD Stadium during the day to sketch and reconnoiter the place. Moses had visited the venue many times over the years and knew the grounds like the back of his heavily creased hand. On the other hand, I only prayed we wouldn't experience any serious wrinkles during the operation. The time of the meeting had been set for 10 PM sharp, meaning about 10:30 or so by Liberian standards. *Godot* was a popular name and timeless experience here.

Our plan called for Moses to drive Mary and me to the locale about an hour before the meet. We would position ourselves a distance away from the actual meeting spot and observe the drama, nothing more. We wanted to see the action firsthand to confirm we had our quarry handily in-hand as well. Jeez, with that mangled sentence, we might as well call this damn operation a slight-of-hand job to keep things simple!

The night watchman manning the main gate to the stadium had already been briefed and bribed. If anything went wrong, he would feign memory loss when the cops questioned him. He understood the drill because he had protected and served for many years too.

Sometimes those who protect and serve got carried away by their own verbosity and crude handiwork.

"Avery, I'm nervous. I've never done anything like this before. I'm still a virgin at these things," Mary spoke for the first time as we headed for the stadium.

To be polite, I didn't comment on her anxiety or sorry condition of her maidenhead. But I did respond to her concerns to alleviate the obvious distress she was experiencing. Maybe I could help her overcome her frigidity too.

"I've done similar things in the past. Of course, nothing too illegal so there's not any reason to worry. Remember Mary, I'm from the government and here to help you," I sarcastically replied to break the tension.

However, I didn't mention that I had swallowed a couple of Valiums and washed them down with a glass of wine before leaving. I had mellowed-out to the point I really didn't give a damn if we were successful or not. Besides, such trivial matters shouldn't be discussed between overly anxious colleagues, especially one who was perpetually horny and the other persistently adverse to sexual intercourse.

"Do you realize the consequences of getting caught if things go to shit?" she replied to my earlier nonsense.

"Sure, we're declared *persona non grata* and shipped home on the next flight to the States. But we both have diplomatic immunity so the authorities can't touch us. Truthfully, I'm more concerned about the possibility of *persona mortis*. I still want to collect my government pension for as long as I can thumb my nose at the miserable, penny-pinching bureaucrats in Washington."

Mary remained silent for the rest of the trip. I fully understood the angst she was experiencing because, if I lived too long, Uncle Sam might run out of money to pay her pension as well. Now that was something to really worry about!

Sometimes those who protect and serve were insightful and caring creatures at heart, right down to their overdrawn checkbooks.

We were waived through the stadium gate by the watchman who intentionally or inadvertently averted his eyes as we drove past. I suspected such behavior was pretty typical for those who had survived the wars. Keeping a low profile and your head lowered must have been a fairly common practice then. Actually, you could never be too careful, even these days.

Moses easily found our designated surveillance spot. Thankfully, he kept the engine and AC running. Even though it was nearly 9 PM, it was still unbearably hot and humid. The noise from our car couldn't be heard from a distance so we didn't worry about being discovered by any bad or good guys. It was difficult to distinguish between the two at times.

We sat back and waited for the actors to arrive since it was almost curtain time. *I hoped it wouldn't be curtains for us,* I joked to myself to relieve my stage fright. The waiting was the very worst part of the operation. We were awaiting the three agents from the National Bureau of Investigations that Mary had recruited for the job.

We were also awaiting the arrival of Amos Brown and whoever he may have hired to back him up in this little drama. It might be difficult to tell the players without a scorecard, as they say. Even without my night vision binoculars, I probably could have recognized Brown from his black and white surveillance photos, but I wouldn't have a clue about the others. I would be virtually colorblind in addition to being clueless. Those conditions made me extremely uncomfortable and I badly needed another ciggie to calm my frayed nerves. Thank God for the curative powers of blind ignorance and strong nicotine!

We watched as a light colored sedan pulled up to the meeting place. I couldn't make out how many occupants were inside the car but Mary confirmed they were the NBI agents she had hired. I felt much better. It was a little before 10 PM, plenty of time before we expected Amos to arrive and he likely would be late. It was expected and customary in these parts. He had to be careful to avoid all of the gangsters that were now emerging from their bolt holes in the Paynesville slums to make a dishonest living by preying on helpless citizens who were foolish enough to venture outside at this hour.

Maybe Charles Darwin would have appreciated the fitting situation. However, the local people didn't and the Community Action Groups didn't either. The groups wanted to be the preeminent predators on the truncated food chain. The extinction of the many bad guys was their primal goal. Only time would tell how things would devolve. Regardless, I wouldn't bet on their long-term survival—the Community Action Groups, I meant. They were badly outnumbered and outgunned by the boys in the hood. *Survival of the fittest* was quickly becoming the national motto of Liberia. No worry, I was positive the phrase would sound less frightening in Latin or Liberian-English.

Our wait ended with the arrival of two motorcycles that zoomed through the gate. They circled the sedan a couple of times and came to a halt on opposite sides. The pillion rider on one cycle got off and stood near the car with his hands folded over his chest. When he finally removed his crash helmet, I could clearly see it was Amos Brown. The bikers had left their engines running for a quick getaway, I guessed.

The three NBI agents got out of the car and approached Amos. After about a minute of talking, the agents took Amos down hard by grabbing him and shoving his face into the pavement. The other agent watched their backs by staring down the bikers who quickly fled the scene. *That turned out to be an easy takedown,* I gloated with much glee.

I jumped out of our vehicle and headed to the commotion. My Glock was safely stuffed down the front of my pants and at the ready. I probably wouldn't need it, but what the Hell, I was a macho sort of guy and innate risk taker. Truthfully, I was scared shitless but I needed to see Amos up-close and personally. I really wanted to know who we were up against in this battle for hearts, minds and oil. Oh, and sustaining Liberian democracy too!

As I approached, I could see the NBI agents trussing-up Amos with pieces of white rope—clothesline no less. They couldn't even afford handcuffs or flex-cuffs to properly secure him. *Jeez, times really are tough,* I thought. As I neared the car, I heard the loud buzz of motorcycles coming in our direction. They sounded like an angry swarm of bees whose hive had just been attacked by a witless kid who'd been blindfolded and told it was a piñata by his so-called buddies. To this day, I've never forgiven them for the cruel, decidedly hurtful prank.

Unlike what I first believed, these guys were no wimps. They were returning to kick some butt and I prayed it wouldn't be the Anglo-American variety. Despite the fact I wasn't Catholic, I still crossed myself for good luck or karma or whatever.

Sometimes those who protect and serve discovered God, religiosity and cowardice at the most inopportune times in life.

The two bikes approached us from opposite directions. The NBI agents were taken by complete surprise, obviously not expecting their return. As I looked up from my prone vantage point on the tarmac, I saw one cyclist drive past the agent who was serving as a guard and lookout. With one swoop from the biker's machete, he decapitated the agent, not quite cleanly but enough where the agent's severed head now drooped onto his chest. Except for the enormous amount of blood, the agent looked like he was in deep meditation with his head fully bowed. But, in truth, the guy never really had a prayer.

The other biker pulled directly up to the car. The sawed-off, double-barreled shotgun was leveled at us on the bike's handle bar. I couldn't gauge its size but it was an effective street sweeper at this range. He couldn't miss or if he did there was a second round already chambered to correct any mistakes. Instinctively, I grabbed my crotch and reached down my pants to retrieve my Glock. As I pulled on its handle, it became entangled in my Jockey shorts. I couldn't get the damn thing out to save my life! This was not only embarrassing but life threatening. I vowed to wear loose-fitting boxers in the future.

As I struggled with my gun and predicament, I heard two short bursts of automatic gunfire ring out from the direction of the nearby shrubs. I looked up and saw the shotgun toting cyclist fall without a sound to the ground. He didn't get up and I could see why. Blood gushed from the center of his T-shirt, pooling around his still body. Whoever did this piece of wet-work was one damn fine shot. It looked as if the rounds had hit the bad guy in a tight cluster in the center of his chest. Ironically, several of the slugs went through the silkscreened red heart on the *Virginia is for Lovers* shirt he was wearing. Without doubt, he was an Americo-Liberian fashionista; a dead one by the looks of things.

The shooter emerged from the bushes and walked to us. Jesus, I recognized the guy! It was Frank Yeaten, the SSS Deputy Director of Operations. *What the hell is going on?* I wondered. Without a word, he dragged the murdered NBI agent's body to the car's trunk and dropped it inside along with the shotgun and M-4 assault rifle that he'd slung over his shoulder. He then helped load Amos Brown into the back seat. Next, Frank propped up the still-running motorcycle and drove off. I suspected he had just scored a trophy for a job well done. He'd certainly earned it in my selfish opinion. He left the bad guy's body lying were it dropped. It would serve as a Liberian lesson that crime didn't pay or that guns do kill. The machete wielding biker was long gone by now, likely to fight or flight another day.

I limped back to our car because my Glock had now retreated to one of my pant legs. Maybe if I waited long enough it would serve as an ankle gun. I quickly jumped in and ordered Moses to get the hell out of here—ASAP or sooner. We trailed the NBI vehicle out the gate and onto Tubman Avenue and got lost in traffic.

As we cruised home, I unzipped my fly and reached inside to remove my gun. Mary looked at me quizzically and began laughing. She asked if I had gotten so excited during the action that I had to relieve myself. I shot her a dirty look and explained that I was simply retrieving my weapon from its hiding spot. That's why it was called a concealed weapon, I brusquely added for clarification.

She asked if that was what men now called the little thingamajig between their legs. Wasn't it called a *cock-up* by the British, she continued to tease? It seemed I couldn't win for losing in the conversation. I kept quiet for a change so I wouldn't lose more face. Regardless, my Glock continued its downward trajectory. I just hoped that I wouldn't shoot myself in the foot as Phil had earlier suggested.

Sometimes those who protect and serve could be so clever and inane at the same times—State Department counterintelligence at its best.

CHAPTER 9

THINGS GET PERSONABLE

Two days after our adventure most of the local rags had reported that the body of an apparent gunshot victim had been found at SKD Stadium. Most stories attributed the killing to a drug deal gone wrong. The victim was well known to the authorities as a small-time dealer and occasional armed robber. There was no sympathy expressed at the guy's passing in any of the articles. Everyone knew that lead poisoning was a common disease (and sometime cure) in Paynesville.

All-in-all, I thought the operation went fairly well. Sure, an NBI agent had been killed in the melee and one bad boy had been permanently put down, but we had captured Amos Brown and that was our objective. Collateral damage sometimes happened in these situations but overall we did well. I always enjoyed accentuating the positive and spinning reality as circumstances and my ego required. I could consciously keep a clear conscience with the best of them.

Mary and I were told that Amos Brown was being held sub

rosa in a cellar at an abandoned army barracks located between Monrovia and Roberts Field. I think that artful statement meant he was being detained under wraps. Regardless, and for some unknown reason, I still kept referring to the international airport as a field. I couldn't help myself since names and habits tended to die hard for us geezers who protected and served in the good old days when men were men and women were glad of it.

Sometimes the memories and sexual fantasies of those who protected and served in the distant past could be very sketchy when it came to distinguishing fact from fiction.

Mary and I agreed that I would do any talking with Amos Brown. She needed to be present to hear what he had to say, if anything, but it was important that Amos not be aware that a woman with a decidedly American accent was involved in our caper. It could jeopardize her safety if Amos was lucky by escaping or wealthy enough to buy his freedom. On the latter point, we made it clear to his jailers that there was a large bonus in store for them at the end of their employment. We also made it abundantly evident that we knew where their families lived. Small carrots and big sticks were never in short supply in Liberia.

We stepped into Amos's holding room. It was small and Spartan without air conditioning. He was blindfolded and tied to a chair behind a rather crude wooden desk. Unfortunately, he couldn't see the situation he was in. I looked at the man with a discerning, professional eye. It appeared that he had suffered some minor injuries during the scuffle at the stadium the other night. The part of his face that was visible was badly bruised in several places and he was missing the fingernail on the pinkie of his left hand. It was healing well by the looks of it. The pair of bloody pliers lying on the table in front of him attested to the accidental nature of his injury. Shame on him for his carelessness! Subcutaneously clipping one's nails during questioning was a nasty, inconsiderate vice that should only be done in a pinch. I didn't bother asking his keepers to remove his trousers so I could check his balls. I was absolutely certain that he had a big set by now.

The U.S. government forbade any employee to engage in any activity that could be construed as torture. It was verboten and totally illegal. That was why Uncle Sam farmed-out its recalcitrant prisoners to friendly allies that had no similar laws, prohibitions or compunctions about the judicious application of physical and emotional measures to loosen tongues and teeth. We were simply following standard government practice with Amos. God bless America and the legal concept of political expediency!

"Amos, you haven't cooperated with your interrogators so I'm told. They asked you questions about why you came to Paynesville, who sent you and what your plans are. We already know you're working for Booku and he has plans to overthrow the Sirleaf government. You are one of his confidantes and trusted lieutenants. I believe you know much that could help us."

I decided not to use the line: *Hi, I'm from the government and here to help you. It had never worked before and wouldn't likely now—why bother?* I thought.

"Why should I help you?" He spoke with some difficulty due to recent dental work, I supposed. "It gains me nothing," he added.

"If I tell you what I may or may not know, Booku will kill me and my family. It won't be a pleasant experience for any of us. Besides, my life insurance's not paid up."

"Why not take our offer that's on the table, figuratively speaking. That would be a green card to the States and $25,000 in greenbacks. It's a fair offer under the circumstances. The alternative is for us to hand you over to the Liberian government. I'm sure it would like to get its hands on you for past, youthful indiscretions. Too bad you're not wanted by The Hague as well."

"Thanks, but I'd rather take my chances with Booku. You never know, he may end up as President of Liberia. Stranger things have happened in this country over the years," he laughingly said.

"By the way, whoever you are, my new, American friend, if

Booku gets his hands on you, he'll skin you alive and laugh at your pain and agony. He has no sense of humor when it comes to those who kidnap his friends. He'll peel you like a banana, one strip of flesh at a time; maybe adding a little fire to your feet for greater comic effect and his enjoyment. He has a rich, perverted imagination and no conscience to limit his actions. You're lucky that large stewpots have gone out of fashion in Africa. Otherwise, asshole, you'd be in a real kettle of fish," he hotly joked.

Amos obviously had a big potty mouth given his coarse language and penchant for oversized cookware.

"Well, let's see how you feel in a few more days as a guest at our establishment. Maybe our hospitality will change your mind," I said as we left him to his own devices—the pliers and other instruments of not-so-friendly persuasion.

I didn't doubt for a second what Amos said about Booku getting his hands on us. We most decidedly would die a horrible death. However, Amos may or may not have understood his fate. Regardless, whether he cooperated or not, he was a dead man sitting. He had seen the NBI agents and jailers faces. They would never let him leave the interrogation site alive. They knew what would happen to them and their families if they mistakenly released him to return to Booku. No, Amos's body would end-up in one of the many swamps as fodder for the crocodiles and other hungry critters that inhabited the places. Nothing went to waste in Liberia these days.

I didn't feel sorry for him in the slightest. With his many sins, he deserved what he would ultimately get. *See you later gator* was the best I could muster under the circumstances. He wouldn't have a chance to say *after awhile crocodile,* I tearfully mused.

Sometimes those who protect and serve subscribed to Einstein's theory of relativity when it came to the irrelevance of others chosen to ride the timeline continuum to oblivion.

I finally caught up with Frank Yeaten as he left the Foreign

Ministry one late afternoon. It wasn't raining at the moment and that was good. In the two weeks I'd been here, it had rained off-and-on every day and/or night. I'd had enough of the waterworks and was thinking about home where it was freezing cold and snowing. *Ok Avery, choose your poison carefully,* I spoke to myself. Whether it was this or whether it was that, the weather choices basically sucked—big time. In any event, I'd hold-off on a decision to stay or go when I wasn't so depressed and under the divisive weathers. I mentally debated such things on assignments when I was terribly bored or frightened to death. In this instance, it must've been my mortality acting up again.

"Frank, do you have a second?" We need to talk. Why were you at the stadium? I certainly appreciate that you saved all of our butts, but why? What are you up to and how did you learn about our operation?"

Since I was on a roll, I thought I might ask him what the meaning of life was too. I didn't because I wasn't sure I wanted to know the answer.

Frank laughed a bit and said I asked a lot of questions for a paunchy, lilywhite foreigner wearing a not-so-fashionable safari suit in darkest Africa.

I was terribly offended by his remark and told him so. It was a leisure suit, damn it! Now I wasn't sure I should have thanked him for saving our lives. Frankly, he had just pressed one of my haberdashery hot buttons, just like the faux pearl ones on my jacket. I wasn't sure I could forgive him for his faux pas but, as a very special agent, I had to put my feelings aside and soldier on. That meant I'd get even for his most egregious slight later. In my profession, payback wasn't a bitch, it was always a Dick!

"Ok, Frank, cut the crap and tell me what's going on with the Rambo stuff. I deserve a straight answer."

"The short answer is I was ordered to," he replied.

"By who?" I shot back.

"By *whom*," he responded. The *whom* is Ellen Johnson-Sirleaf, the President of Liberia."

I was stunned by what he had just said. Frank was not only a crack shot but a strict grammarian as well! The Sirleaf part was sort of interesting too.

"She briefed me on your mission and ordered me to watch your back. I've been shadowing you since your arrival in Monrovia. By the way, ditch the safari suit and buy a dashiki. At least then you'll look like a normal tourist instead of something out of 1970's sitcom."

I was quickly taking a dislike to this most rude Liberian. But I also wondered how I'd look in a dashiki. Who knew? Maybe it would be suitable for me.

"Also your tradecraft was a bit sloppy the other night Avery. Luckily, Amos didn't pick up on your mistakes. If he had, things might have turned out much worse."

First it was my dress, then my speech and now my modus operandi. Was nothing sacred with this guy? My self-esteem was heading south. However, he may have had a point with the tradecraft quip. We should have been more careful. Perhaps we should have sent Amos Brown a pleasant diplomatic note from the U.S. embassy inviting him for tea and a chat. That would have been the typical Foreign Service solution for dealing with vicious thugs bent on overthrowing a democratically elected government.

Would you like another cookie Mr. Brown? They're all half-baked in Washington, my dear.

"By the way, the president appreciates your government's help with Booku. We don't have the resources to put a stop to his madness. Moreover, the whole issue's a political hot potato because Taylor still has support among the people. The Sirleaf government has to be very careful not to stir the pot too much and rile up the people that support his, or in this case, his surrogate's return to power either legally or by force. That would be too messy and could lead to uprisings and outright civil strife. Madame President needs to walk a fine line until our institutions are strengthened and democracy is more fully embraced by the citizenry. We still have a ways to go."

"No one other than the president knows I'm involved in this thing. She swore me to secrecy and I will respect her wish at all costs, to include my own life. You see Avery, Booku and I have some history between us and none of it is good. He tried to kill me some years ago. To make a very long story short, Booku accused me of plotting to overthrow Taylor. It was all nonsense but paranoia ruled in those days. I was an officer in the army at the time and assigned to the Monrovia barracks. One night Booku's SSS goons paid me a visit. I was taken to the Executive Mansion and ushered into Taylor's private suite. He was sitting on a sofa with his feet propped on a coffee table. Booku stood behind him with a smug look on his face. Taylor looked laid back and relaxed. I was wrong. He turned out to be highly agitated and angry."

"I stood at attention while he accused me of treachery and disloyalty. The harangue went on for a full five minutes and he became more enraged with each passing one. He paced the room and delivered-up vile accusations of my complicity in some sort of plot. I didn't have any idea how I could have ended-up before him. Like everyone else, I was very circumspect in my actions and speech when it came to Taylor. Even the slightest criticism of him or his regime could make you disappear. Someone must have passed my name out of spite or money or whatever. That's how things worked in those days. If you didn't like someone and wanted him permanently removed, you simply reported him to the authorities as a spy or traitor. The SSS would take things from there. There was no recourse or remorse. Torture would bring out the truth of the allegation—whatever truth was preordained by the interrogators."

"You remember the saying about your life passing before your eyes at times like this? It's absolutely true. I recalled key events in my past, especially the ones I wasn't particularly proud of. I prayed for my life while standing there. I was so nervous I ended up pissing myself. The urine ran freely down the front of my uniform trousers. I peed so much that a small puddle formed at my feet."

"Taylor started laughing at my embarrassing plight and sight. He laughed so hard that he choked at times. He then turned to Booku and said that anyone who would piss his pants didn't have the courage to overthrown him. Sissies didn't plot coups or standup to strong men. He then dismissed me with a derisive wave of his arm. In his mind, I wasn't worth an execution. That would be too honorable for an obvious coward and mama's boy who couldn't hold his own."

"As I left his office, he shouted that I should wear a nappy, or diaper as you Americans call them, next time I was in his presence. I was thoroughly humiliated by the experience but still alive. I preferred living to the alternative but it all depends on the size of one's ego and bodily functions."

"I wasn't offered a ride back to the barracks but I did receive transfer orders the following week to a military depot in southern Liberia, close to the border with the Ivory Coast. It was considered a permanent retirement home for those who had crossed Taylor. One would be sent there, never to return. Within a few months of arriving, one would simply disappear. Of course, the official rumor mill would report that so-and-so had fled across the border to the Ivory Coast and was now living the good life. More likely, what was left of his or her body could be found washed-up on shore. "

"I disobeyed the order knowing the consequences. Instead, I hid out in Monrovia relying on the help of close friends and relatives to get by. I laid low for the next 18 months until Taylor fled office. I remember the day he left the country since most of us were able to get our first breath of fresh air in four years. It was though a dark cloud had been lifted from us and we finally felt free. I don't want my country to go back to those days of fear and repression. That's why it's so critical to put an end to Booku and/or his plot. Either option will do because we don't have that much time I'm afraid."

I was beginning to warm up to Frank despite his earlier, hurtful comments. He had undergone a traumatizing experience with Taylor and lived to tell the tale. But he was no sissy or mama's boy by any means. While he might suffer from incontinence, we were on the Dark Continent at the moment so his bladder disorder didn't make any difference to me, grammatically or geographically speaking.

"Let's exchange cell phone numbers so we better coordinate our activities. It's your show but I'm duty-bound to cover your ass. More importantly, I will be able to finally get some sleep instead of chasing you all around town. Call me if you want to get together. Just dial my number and hit the callback button. I'll do the same if I need to see you. We'll meet here at the MFA. Nobody will pay us any attention. People know about your purported assignment with the SSS and I practically live here."

"Take care Avery and remember to buy some new threads my man," Frank said as he headed for his car in the parking lot.

Walking the short distance to my apartment, I pondered the significance of Frank's role in our operation and his chiding me on my poor dressing skills. I had much to think about. I guessed that my black wingtips and bruised ego would go with just about anything Liberia had to offer.

Sometimes those who protect and serve couldn't countenance the little cruelties visited upon them by more fashion conscious colleagues.

CHAPTER 10

POISONOUS POTPOURRI

Amos Brown had kept mum. That was the word used by his minders to describe his intransigence and perhaps his stubbornness as well. Regardless, he wasn't talking. His usefulness was quickly slipping away and he couldn't grasp the consequences of his silence. He also couldn't grasp the consequences of blabbing his head off. They would be one-in-the same in his case. Amos was destined to serve as a carryout meal for the black lagoons many ravenous creatures. Even his Mum wouldn't be able to recognize her son afterwards. His remains soon would easily fit in a medium-sized, plastic Glad bag if such things were available here. Probably not since there just wasn't that much Joy left in the country either.

However, Mama Brown would finally get her due and just reward for birthing a loathsome bastard! Jeez, hadn't she heard about birth control or, better yet, abortion? A forcible forceps delivery in the later part of her third trimester could have worked wonders for the people of Liberia. Just yank the cancerous growth from her womb and plop it in the garbage. The village's feral dogs would clean up the mess in short order.

Sometimes those who protect and serve gladly enjoyed using purple prose to describe sanguine events.

I wasn't quite ready to terminate Amos's life with extreme prejudice since he still might have some utility to us later on; maybe as a bargaining chip with Booku. Maybe he would eventually talk and reveal something useful. Maybe he could be turned into low-grade fertilizer for the grounds of Executive Mansion. *Now that would be a fitting end for the piece of dung,* I thought. But who really knew when all was said and done? I certainly didn't. I freely admitted that I had shocked myself with what I had just said and almost done. *Where did my little bit of largesse and altruism spring from?* I wondered. Again, I was confused and totally clueless, at least until I mulled these things over in my muddled mind.

Avery, you're going soft in the head again, my mind spoke. I mean the one above your shoulders dickhead, it immediately clarified. Get the dirty deed over with dude. Put it behind you and move on. It isn't the worst thing you've done for your Uncle Sam. Do you want me to remind you of other, more coldblooded things you've done during your long career with DS? Let's take a slow stroll together down memory lane my cerebral friend. No? I didn't think so. Bite the bullet wimp and focus on the future. Much needs to be done to succeed in your mission. I can guarantee you that Mother State won't be happy if you screw things up again. You'll be out on your ass clipping coupons and drinking cheap bottles of wine with screw-tops if you don't make the right decision this time. Think it over very carefully Avery. If you have any questions, just give me a quick thought. Put your trust in me, bud. I'm from the government and here to help you!

I wasn't so sure about what my nasty, devilish mind had just suggested. My better angels refused to come to the fore or my aid to counterbalance the mindless argument. Perhaps I'd simply forgotten to take my meds again. However, what I did know was that Amos Brown wasn't going anywhere fast, but then again neither were we. We still needed a bold next step to counteract Booku and his insidious plans for the downtrodden people of Liberia. I was terribly worried about our prospects since it didn't seem that either God or my psychotropic drugs were on our side at the moment.

Sometimes comforting, redeeming salvations were tough to swallow for those who protect and serve.

I found out the mosquitoes were large and especially vicious in Monrovia. But Malaria wasn't the only worry here. More to the point, I had forgotten to take my prophylactics and wear my bulletproof vest. Memory loss could be a real killer for the thoughtless and forgetful.

I had Moses drop me at the entrance to my compound after a long day of thinking-up ways to stop or at least slow down Booku. My skull session with myself left me with a huge headache. I was always mindful of my poor debating skills and could never win any side of these internal arguments. However, I had some ideas to share with Mary and get her blessing to go ahead with them. I hoped she wouldn't laugh because they were a little bit unorthodox. Generally, orthodoxy was a desired trait in DS, Hebraic or otherwise. That was because it involved conformity, consensus and no thinking outside of the box. However, circumcision was optional for us gentiles with foreskin, unless you really screwed-up. That was when the organization's sharp knifes came out.

As I approached the entrance, I heard a whizzing sound next to my right ear and a ping on the metal gate. As I turned around to see what was happening, I felt a slight jolt to my chest. I looked down and saw a two-inch piece of something sticking out of my breast pocket. Jesus, my box of Marlboro reds had just been attacked! More importantly, I realized that cigarette smoking had just saved my life. Who said that cancer sticks were bad for your health? The AMA should tell my story on its website to counter all of the phony medical hype. Maybe I could be a poster boy for the Brown and Williamson Tobacco Company. I'd gladly work for trade.

I bent over to pick up the object that had just dropped to the ground. I carefully scanned the area behind me and saw nothing unusual. *What the hell was going on?* I wondered.

I gingerly collected the small objects and placed them in my nearly empty cigarette box. I suspected what they were but needed to urgently contact Frank to confirm my theory of the crime. I had his number on speed-dial and pressed the send, followed by the call-back, button. I couldn't wait to see him. Absence and attempted murder made the heart grow fonder. Someone was out to get me and I didn't need three guesses to figure out who or whom.

Frank avoided touching the darts and moved them around with the tip of his pen. "Do you know what these are?" he eventually asked.

"Yep, those are the things that almost killed me this afternoon." Jeez, did Frank think I was totally naïve and ignorant at the same time about such things? Yeah, maybe he did and just maybe he was right.

"You're right, they're reed darts shaped and sharpened to a fine point. Luckily, you didn't get the point. If you had, we wouldn't be talking now."

"My hunch is they've been soaked in a fast-acting poison, probably alligator gut. That's a very popular and inexpensive potion in these parts. Usually, it's administered as a fine powder and placed in food. In that form, the victim suffers severe gastrointestinal problems and dies within 24 hours. In your case, the poison would have immediately entered your bloodstream. You maybe had an agonizing hour or so before dying. Alligator gut is a bilious, galling way to die. I've witnessed its effects on several occasions and I can assure you they're not pleasant."

"You probably don't know but pygmies shoot these darts from a blowgun made from a length of bamboo. It's an accurate, effective weapon in the right hands."

"You mean I was ambushed by a pygmy? That's absurd!"

"Avery, the short answer is no," Frank snickered.

Jesus, this guy was punning about my near-death experience! Was there no respect for the feelings of middle-aged, paunchy federal bureaucrats anymore? I could have gotten more sympathy from the zombie hall-walkers in Main State, damn him to Hell.

"The closest pygmy tribes are located in the rainforests of Gabon, Cameroon and the Congo, about a thousand miles from Liberia. You were the victim of a rebel tactic that was successfully employed during the wars. A number of the rebels were trained in the use of the blowgun and sent to the frontlines to quietly kill government sentries before a surprise attack. It worked well and the government troops were scared to death to stand guard."

"Old habits and skills die hard sometimes. By the way, there's currently no shortage of bamboo and reed in the country. These things flourished after the war because they didn't require planting and cultivation. They just grew of their own accord. Those are perfect crops for Liberians who wouldn't bother to plant a seed these days. We have extremely fertile land that has ideal growing conditions. Yet, we are a lazy people who wouldn't stoop to such labor when international organizations are willing to feed us. Ask anyone, it's true. It's a sad commentary about my country."

"But back to your situation, somebody is sending you a pointed message and we both know who it is. Avery, you need to keep your head down and watch your step in the future; these guys play for keeps."

Sometimes those who protect and serve occasionally bent over and ungraciously kissed their ass goodbye.

Mary didn't salute, at least not right away. I'd run-up my ideas on the flagpole of her credulity and she stared at several of the pennants for a long time. None were flown upside down but she was still skeptical at first. Eventually, she warmed up to most of them and even acknowledged that they might work under the circumstances. But her initial reaction wasn't particularly cordial.

"The Wizard of Oz? What in hell are you talking about?" Mary exclaimed. "Are you out of your frigging mind?"

I purposely avoided answering her last question and pressed-on by explaining what I actually had on my mind.

"Sure, don't you remember the scene where the Wicked Witch of the West skywrites: *'Surrender Dorothy or die.'*"

"We're going to do something similar to Booku in order to disrupt his plans by discrediting him and disenfranchising his supporters. We're going to mount a robust psych-op and disinformation campaign against him," which I cackled to support my credibility.

Mary and I were sitting in my apartment at the Sea Suites and drinking our Zinfandel. I had gained her admittance to the back gate of the property by giving the guard on duty my old Timex. I would buy a new one later on Uncle Sam's time and dime. Mostly, I could be very watchful of other people's money.

"Okay, here are some specific suggestions. First, we carpet bomb all of Lofa County and hope we get lucky. That just might pull the rug from under his feet," I joked to a less than rapt audience of one. Damn, I could be so amusing and foolish at the same time! And I wasn't kidding in the slightest.

"Seriously, here's what I think would knock him off balance and put him on the ropes at least for awhile. It wouldn't be a fatal blow, but would slow-up and set-back his plans until we delivered the coup de grace—a sucker punch to the groin to bring him to his knees and our arms."

"I see an escalating campaign with the following scenarios. Step one is to distribute flyers of Booku offering a reward of $100,000 for his capture—dead or alive. *Dead* would be preferable since it would save many hundreds of thousands of dollars in transferring him to The Hague, holding him for trial, paying his legal costs and incarcerating him in prison for a very long time. The buck would stop in Liberia if I had my way," I racially and inadvertently punned. Well, perhaps not. Booku's skin color was whiter than mine but I chided myself just the same for the off-color remark. But the truth was that I often couldn't discriminate one from another since greenbacks only came in one color.

"I'm sure the world's taxpayers would appreciate the frugality of the conundrum," I quickly added to restore my smug superiority and assuage my White Man's guilt complex.

"Avery, $100,000 is way too much money to offer," Mary interrupted. "Save Uncle Sam a few bucks and only offer $25K. That's more than enough to entice someone to turn on Booku, if we can find somebody so inclined. Remember that he still has much support in his strongholds and he's a fearsome figure among the people."

It appeared that Mary's mixed blood couldn't be held in check either. I now felt fully vindicated as well as assuaged by her comments. I lit a cigarette to assuage my nicotine craving. My vindication as a habitual smoker would have to wait another time.

"Okay, that's fine. $25,000 it will be. I'll arrange for the printing of the handbills and come up with some verbiage explaining why his followers should drop the dime on him. The $25K alone is a lot of dimes in my opinion. I'll use his photograph, the one I filched from Booku's SSS personnel file."

"Mary, we need to setup a phone number for people to call to report Booku's whereabouts. We need to record all incoming calls and see if any have value. In any case, we're going to receive a shitload of them—good, bad and ugly. Your friends at the NSA should be able to establish a drop-line with the Lonestar cell phone folks. They seem to be plugged into the company so it shouldn't be a problem."

Mary nodded in the affirmative while I continued speaking.

"Next on the list of things to do is to create a blitz newspaper attack on Booku, recounting his many crimes and highlighting the fact that he's currently wanted by the International Court of Justice. We'll pay for stories to be planted that argue for his capture to stand trial for his misdeeds. This action will be a little tricky but I think Frank can pull it off through his contacts in the media who are pro-Sirleaf. I'll talk to him."

"Lastly, we'll up the ante by using friendly radio stations to broadcast unfriendly pieces about Booku. They'll report false information about his current activities in Liberia to further stoke the fire. Again, we'll need Frank's help to make it happen but I think it's easily doable since money will be on the table. Many people, even those living in the bush, have battery-operated radios. I don't believe we'll have any problem getting our message out to the natives in the hinterlands. Let's see if we can get a couple of stations in Sierra Leone to cooperate as well. They have no love for the guy considering what Taylor and his bunch did to the country during the civil wars. Since he's been spotted from time-to time crossing the border with Liberia, maybe we can put the pressure on him to hole-up in one location for at least awhile. It's worth a shot."

"However, one thing that we need to be careful of is creating a trail that could lead back to Sirleaf or the ambassador at the U.S. embassy. Let's keep the bread crumbs to a minimum. We need to keep both of them out of this stuff if we can or for as long as we can."

"Avery, I like your plan. It's a good move in the right direction. It will likely create confusion among Booku's loyalists and maybe, just maybe, lead us to him. In any event, he'll be looking over his shoulder more often."

"As you were talking, I thought of something else we might do to box-in Booku and cause him to make a mistake that will bring him out of hiding," Mary mentioned. "I want to give it more thought but it could fit nicely with the disinformation campaign you've just outlined. It's something that will likely put me at odds with my African heritage and sworn oaths but I'm willing to do anything to bring down Booku. The fucker really needs to die! I'll fill you in later after I've fleshed things out a bit in my mind."

Mary had just piqued my curiosity about what was on her mind. So much so, that I asked if she wanted to stay overnight to discuss her quandary. I thought *quandary* referred to someone's sexual kinks and desires but it turned out that I was wrong. She politely declined my generous offer for bed and breakfast, finished her drink and said goodnight. I escorted her out the back gate of the compound. As I did, I could easily see the luminescence of night guard's new watch in the darkness. I wondered if he could tell time. No matter, I wasn't sure what time it was either in terms of our investigation.

Sometimes those who protect and serve simply needed a good licking to keep on ticking.

CHAPTER 11

JUJU JAMBOREE

Mary objected to my idea to attach a banner to the plane that dropped the leaflets all over Lofa County. I thought *Surrender Booku or die, merci beaucoup* was a nice, polite touch. However, Mary thought I was a bit touched. She won the day and argument. God, she could be so touchy at times! *Okay, touché mon ami,* I thought in my best French.

Our campaign was moving ahead nicely. So far, things had gone to plan. Frank had successfully recruited several newspaper editors to lambast and lampoon Booku in the print media. It would take a few days for the newspapers to arrive in Booku's neighborhood but once they did he would be furious. He'd undoubtedly cancel his subscriptions. We had yet to pull the trigger on the radio broadcasts, holding that punch behind our back for the moment. I admitted that I really liked the manly talk of guns, especially when associated with Mr. Booku. It suggested strong action and false bravado. We needed both things right now to see us through our mission. I hoped we wouldn't have to bite the bullet or swallow our gun when all was done. Such acts were too orally uncomfortable and embarrassing.

Frank and Mary were poring over the voice messages coming

into our dedicated phone line at Lonestar. So far nothing of consequence had been reported. However, much inconsequential stuff had been accumulated. Many callers vented their anger against the Sirleaf government and its obvious attempt to stop Booku's rise to power. Many more callers solicited money for various causes, invariably their own, charitable ones.

Several women proposed marriage or at least sponsorship to whoever might be listening. They figured that if 25 thousand dollars was being offered as a reward, there must be more money where that came from. Deep pockets, a generous disposition and a big Johnson were sought-after attributes by many Liberian ladies. However, the Johnson part clearly indicated they only wanted to date well-endowed Americo-Liberians. Regardless, Scandinavian names must be very popular here.

This nationality nonsense was getting too confusing, a mish-mash of American, Liberian and Scandinavian. *Where was I?* I rhetorically asked no one in particular. *Liberia, shit-for-brains!* I was rhetorically answered by no one in particular. I didn't particularly like the snotty response.

Sometimes those who protect and serve got seriously derailed in relating geographic locales after losing their train of thought.

I got the call late in the afternoon. I had just finished my nap so it didn't interrupt my nearly-daily constitutional. I especially enjoyed its long bill of rights. I was a true hellion when it came to defending them. Jeez, didn't consistency have to be consistent to work properly? At my age, I badly needed my sleep, wine and cigarettes but not necessarily in that order. I scored with the women in my dreams so I was getting my daily ration of real and vicarious creature comforts and notional vices. I was a happy camper and a thoroughly dissolute person until I answered the phone. For what it was worth, I continued to remain resolutely dissolute during and after the call too.

I fumbled with the phone before saying hello. My telephone

etiquette was sorely lacking and remiss and I severely chided myself for my clumsiness. I simply couldn't abide dropped calls, accidental or otherwise. I listened closely to what the caller had to say.

"Mr. Dick, this is Merci Beaucoup. I suspect you know who I am so let's not play games. I want Amos Brown released from your custody. If you do, I might let you live. If you don't, you know your fate. You almost met it the other day in front of your apartment."

"I'm not someone to screw around with. You've likely heard the same from others. I'm offering you a chance to live. By the way, I know what you're up to with your little mind games. They're pathetic, feeble attempts to stop the inevitable from happening. You can't do a damn thing to slow up my plan. Its outcome has been foretold by the juju men of my country."

"You may not believe in such things given your Western disdain for magic. But in Africa it's real and powerful. You need to tell the Oma that her days are numbered. Yours are too if you don't behave and do as I say. I'm not joking. You have 24 hours to release Amos Brown unharmed. Otherwise you'll suffer the consequences. Mr. Dick, a quick death by poison will seem a humane act after I get through with you."

The phone then abruptly went dead. I prayed for a better ending for our little team. I didn't have a chance to get a word in edgewise with the guy. If I could have interrupted his monologue, I would have teased and taunted him to further piss him off. Maybe something like: *nah, nah, nah—you can't catch me Mr. Smarty Pants.* Perhaps something a little more masculine would have worked better. Regardless, he'd get my strong message just the same. I refused to be intimidated by a ruthless, insane ghoul with a lot of years of combat experience—scared shitless, yes, intimidated, no.

However, the takeaway message from Booku's diatribe was that we were getting to him with our psych-op antics. Despite his blustering, he was feeling the heat. We had snatched his best bud, Amos Brown, and now we were starting to play in his own backyard. If nothing else, he must be losing face among his supporters. *If he lost much more, he'd be translucent,* I shamelessly chuckled.

Even his reference to the Oma was transparent. I knew what the word meant—*old woman* in Liberia-speak. Among the people it was the common, respectful name for Ellen Sirleaf. It seemed that even Booku showed some respect for her personage and position. That would only last as long as her execution at his hands or until she hastily fled the country. Those would be her only options unless we came through for her.

There was something else that was both transparent and opaque at the same time. We had a leak on our team, a gusher by the looks of it. Booku knew my personal cell phone number and where I lived. The fact we had a leak was obvious but his or her identity was still a shrouded mystery. I had no idea who it could be since only relatively few people knew of our mission and the team's identities.

There were only a handful of Washington bureaucrats who were privy to our true reason for being in Liberia. I believed that *privy* was a wholly appropriate word for those who leak. That was because of those civil servants who couldn't or wouldn't keep things zipped tight. Diarrhea of the mouth was a constant worry around the office water coolers—Tourette's syndrome even more so. But I didn't think the leak came from Washington.

More likely it was someone here who had betrayed us and was reporting to Booku. By my count, only the President of Liberia, Frank Yeaten, the U.S. ambassador, Mary Tambo and me were permitted the use of the privy—for official purposes only of course. The NBI agents and Amos's jailers weren't witting to most of what we had done or planned. They weren't the likely culprits.

I fully trusted Mary, but Frank much less so. I still wasn't convinced he was true red, white and blue; the colors of his nation's flag. He wrapped himself in it too often to suit me. As for Ellen Sirleaf and the American ambassador, it was possible they might have slipped-up and inadvertently dropped a word or two about the operation. However, I couldn't imagine them mentioning our names under any circumstances. They knew the score and personal consequences of such a disclosure. No, I believed our spy was someone who was close by and watching our every move—at least mine. I'd have to be more careful in watching my step and back.

I later briefed Mary on Booku's telephone call. She agreed that he sounded like he was on the defensive but that didn't make him any less dangerous, only more so. He was angry and would strike-out at the slightest provocation. She emphasized that none of us were safe when he was in a fit of blind rage if the stories about his eyesight were true.

According to Mary's take, he would try to get what he wanted at all costs even if that meant risking his own life. He didn't care because he had the African gods on his side. In his own mind, that meant he was invincible and couldn't fail. She mentioned that his personality was textbook megalomania, right out of a chapter in DSM-IV. Regardless, a sociopathic, megalomaniac (with the clinical signs of bipolar disorder) made for a formidable opponent in anyone's book, she concluded.

However, I took a slightly different view. I believed his little snit and temper tantrum might cause him to make some not-so-little mistakes that could play into our hands. *Hell, who doesn't suffer from the occasional, minor and emotional upset these days?* I asked myself. I didn't wait for an answer this time and quickly moved on to other thoughts. As obvious, I enjoyed accentuating the positive in mostly hopeless, dire situations. Pollyanna was always one of my favorite boyhood heroines.

Sometimes those who protect and serve described their adversaries little quirks and idiosyncrasies in less than flattering terms.

Given the leak, I ordered Amos Brown to be moved to another location. It was a prudent move under the circumstances. That was an odd thing for me to do since I'd never been a prude before.

Perhaps I could have been mistaken for a prune with my badly wrinkled skin but I was never intentionally prudish. Maybe I was just incredibly modest instead. That was a much more acceptable explanation.

In any case, what I proposed to Mary was not immodest in the slightest even though I wanted her to bare all. After some gentle coaxing, she gave me what I wanted to hear. I was totally shocked by what she revealed to me. Who knew what evil lurked in the hearts of men—or women for that matter? Well, Mary and her shadow knew for damn sure! It had bothered her for a long time but now she was ready to disclose some dark secrets to further our cause. I ended up admiring her greatly for what she told me in the strictest of confidence. I vowed never to betray her trust unless expediency or my forgetfulness dictated otherwise. She was one tough lady who had been through much in her earlier years and deserved respect, along with my awkward, lustful advances.

"Avery, I mentioned at our last meeting, the one where you asked me to stay the night, I had an idea to ratchet-up the pressure on Booku. Basically, a continuation of the campaign we've been waging but something that will really shake his tree and confidence."

"I remember that you had an idea but don't recall hitting you up. Maybe it was the wine or my senility that caused the memory lapse. Not sure which at my age," I brazenly lied. *Admit nothing and hope for the best outcome.* That was the DS mantra. Plausible denial was everything in my profession but she easily saw through my bullshit.

She laughed at my obvious lie, sidestepping my prior, indiscreet suggestion for sex. I appreciated her discretion and benevolence. However, my testosterone level was still soaring but my self-esteem consistently hovered in the lowest of numbers. Other than humping Mary or pumping Avery Junior, I didn't know how to get out of my slump and relieve my inner demons.

"Okay, whatever, but I need to tell you a few things about myself when I was growing up. I'm not particularly proud of them but they happened and I can't erase them from my mind. My story is a little long so bear with me. Towards the end, I'll explain how we can use Booku's unshakable belief in African magic against him."

"My family lived in Grand Bassa County in the southeast part of the country. Not surprising, they were members of the Bassa tribe and so were I and my younger brother. Avery, keep in mind that there are many indigenous tribes in Liberia. They sometimes get along but often they don't. I can't explain the phenomenon but I'm sure it's the same today as when I was a kid. Alliances with other tribes are formed and then broken for a variety of reasons, usually petty ones by Western standards. But that's the way it is for better or worse. It's a very confusing situation given the numerous intermarriages and extended families that exist in this country."

"I'm not even sure where things stand with the Bassa these days. However, I do know that I have many brothers and sisters who are part of my extended family. But I don't know who most are. For example, if a married man dies, his brother or cousin takes in his wife and children. Multiply that situation plus normal procreation and you'll get a sense of the numbers. They're huge. Elder tribesmen keep track of *who's who* with elaborate, detailed genealogical charts; mostly in their heads in the oral tradition but sometimes written down."

"I'm going to relate things in a more-or-less chronological order but they don't necessarily need to be for purposes of my idea. I'll share these things with you and expect you to honor my honesty, shame and hope for a better Liberia. Several are embarrassing and I'm reluctant to tell you my secrets. However, I must so you'll better understand our societies and customs. It was a big part of my life and heritage until I moved to the States. Those things still hold me captive to my past in many ways."

"Avery, Mother Africa is an ancient continent and basic things tend to change very slowly, if ever. One summer when I was seven years old, my parents sent me to visit my grandmother who lived in the bush. I adored her and looked forward to visiting when school was out for summer vacation. I quickly made friends among the village children and I was very happy. I played from sunup to sundown and had a wonderful time with my loving grandmother. One day, my grandmother woke me up very early. That was unusual. Maybe something special was happening in the village this day, I excitedly thought."

"There was, but not something I would like. My grandmother took my hand and we walked several hundred yards to a clearing in the jungle. There were about six people waiting there. I was terribly confused and frightened at that point. What was going on? I wondered. Where were my playmates? I looked at my grandmother for comfort but she turned away from me."

"Two people lifted me and placed me on what I can only describe as a sawhorse with a broad back and curved end. My legs were spread and kept propped open by leather thongs attached to the bottom of my wannabe horse. My panties were then cut away and I started screaming. *What was happening?* My mind raced as it spoke to me and I was frightened to death. My grandmother hushed me when I screamed. The only thing she said over and over again was I was becoming a woman. I had no idea what she was talking about. I was hysterical and couldn't stop yelling and crying. I begged them to stop but they didn't. A man approached and touched me between my legs. He told me not to worry and then removed my clitoris with a sharp knife. I had just undergone a cliterectomy at the hands of my grandmother."

"My cries for help went unanswered. The man took some ointment and spread it over my vagina. It seemed to stanch the heavy bleeding I was experiencing. The blood had run down my thighs, over the horse and onto the ground. I was in shock at that point and don't remember much after that. Over the next 10 days, my grandmother attended to my wound, cleaning it day and night. I kept asking her what had happened but she never answered except to say

I would understand later. She was right. I did understand later and I was furious. I never played again with my new friends."

"I learned much later that my father was adamant that I undergo the ritual. My mother begged him not to because she knew the results having undergone the same procedure as a child. I've never forgiven my father for his misguided act of genital mutilation."

"If you think these things don't happen today, you're very wrong. Female circumcisions are regularly performed in Africa every day. Children are subjected to the most despicable cruelties. Why do the parents do it? That's the question. They do it because it's customary, stupid and ignorant custom and nothing more. If men were being castrated, you better believe the practice would be stopped in short order. But of course the two things aren't similar. Men couldn't procreate without balls. Women can still procreate with a missing clit. It's as simple as that. Men believe that intercourse shouldn't be pleasurable—at least for the woman. More importantly, the barbaric act will keep them from seeking-out other men or so they believe. It's all about having children and creating chattel in the male-dominated society."

"Sure, circumcision's illegal but so what. The laws aren't enforced, and even if they are, the perpetrators only get a light slap on the wrist for what they've done. It's an obscene practice that has brought misery to those who have been forced to suffer the procedure. The custom needs to be stopped to save our children. It's an abomination that still exists within our country and elsewhere in the world."

"Avery you've made a couple of lame passes since we met. It's not that I'm not attracted to balding, older white guys. It's because I can't enjoy sex like a normal woman. I simply don't get the tingle between my thighs that other women experience. I wish it weren't so but it is. I'll never get married because I couldn't subject my husband to my physical disability, my terrible secret and shame."

Mary started crying and I put an arm around her to comfort her. She had really drawn the shit card in the game of life. I truly felt sorry for her and wished I could do more to make her feel better. Here was a beautiful, smart woman who couldn't enjoy one of the most natural acts in life. Things weren't fair to put it mildly. I apologized to her for my fumbling, insensitive advances on her womanhood.

I was now behaving like a gentleman because my earlier attempts to exploit her vulnerabilities by not-so-cleverly soliciting sex had failed miserably. Jeez, I could be such a dick at times! I was so distraught that I immediately wanted to change my name, my first not last. Avery was such a wimpy handle. Truthfully, I wanted to hide under the nearest rock and hibernate for the rest of my days. That's how badly I felt about Mary and her emotional pain.

However, I still wondered if she might give me a blowjob later tonight. It wasn't out of the question. Why not? The act didn't involve her pussy so what was the big deal? I'd have to wait and see how she was feeling later, I supposed. Okay, I could play the waiting game too if there was the possibility of some head-action afterwards. I also wondered if she had any qualms about anal intercourse. I wasn't very picky, just being especially considerate of her sensitive, vaginal condition. Christ, I could be so damn caring at times that it scared the hell out of me!

After a few minutes, she regained her composure and continued to tell her story. I was still reeling from her revelations and my prospects for hot sex later. My eyes moistened at the thought of what she had endured. My penis watered a little too in anticipation of things that might come. Being a standup guy, I told her I was suffering from an allergy, a sinus condition caused by the Liberian weather. I purposely didn't mention my moist boxers. It seemed that I'd just developed a strong reaction to African stupidity, cruelty and potential piece of ass. But I avoided telling her about my extreme state of horniness. Better to leave some things unsaid but hopefully not undone in the end.

Sometimes those who protect and serve were sensitive, caring human beings who still needed to fuck their brains out in every way possible.

CHAPTER 12

A FEMME FATALE CONFESSES ALL

"Avery, are you familiar with Freemasonry?" The question took me aback.

"Sure they're the people that are conspiring to control the world brick-by-brick through constructive works. Am I close?" I was truly mortarfied by my less-than-concrete response. I just couldn't help myself or Mary's telling of the story.

"Very funny," Mary sarcastically quipped. "For the ignorant in the audience, the Freemasons are an old, fraternal organization dedicated to helping others of their membership and the general public. The organization does many good deeds around the world that get little or no publicity. That's the way they want things because it's a secretive society as well. There's nothing evil or strange about it despite what the conspiracy theorists claim. The only thing that bothers me is that's it a *male only* organization."

"If you don't know anything about the Freemasons, you'll obviously know even less about the Order of the Eastern Star. That would put you in the negative category in your sparse lexicon of American history or African history for that matter, Avery."

I ignored her putdown and blow to my fragile ego. Of course, she was right. I didn't have a clue about such things.

"The Order of the Eastern Star is an affiliated organization of the Freemasons. It's organized much along the same lines and has a similar hierarchy, set of rituals and penchant for secrecy. Its purpose and mission are also very similar to freemasonry. It's predominately female in origin and membership although it now admits men. Women are more progressive in their thinking than men."

"This is all very interesting but what does any of this have to do with bringing down Mr. Booku?"

"Be patient, I'm getting there but you need to hear this stuff for perspective and context. You also may learn something in the process."

"But the quick answer to your question is the Sande."

I couldn't see how Little Orphan Annie's pooch had anything to do with the conversation. I was now dogged by serious doubt and Mary's state of mind and sense of direction.

"Mary, what are you talking about?" It was my turn to question her sanity.

"The Sande is a secret, female African society that has existed at least a hundred years. Like the Order of the Eastern Star, it has a male counterpart called the Poro. Both are pan-African organizations but their numbers are greatest in the West African countries where they originated."

"Both societies transcend geographic and tribal boundaries. That is one of their purposes. They have created a human infrastructure throughout West Africa that is dedicated to hard work and good deeds. Governments rise and fall and generally have no impact on everyday life here. They're all considered corrupt and ineffectual. The Sande and Poro fill an important void in people's lives by providing purpose, historical continuity, religiosity and upholding the longstanding rules of bush law. There are few social nets for people to fall back on. That's not how things work on this continent. Social and protective services are provided by family and relatives, sometimes by the tribal elders, but most often through the efforts of the Poro and Sande."

"That's why I earlier mentioned the Freemasons and Order of the Eastern Star to illustrate there are similar organizations at work here. Some have even suggested that the Poro and Sande are offshoots of the Freemasons. I'm not sure, but it's interesting to note that in the late 1700s a freeborn African American named Prince Hall, along with sixteen other black men, was inducted into the Boston Freemason lodge."

"Prince Hall became disillusioned with the lodge's politics, especially by the fact that it wouldn't publically speak out against slavery. He and some of his followers petitioned the Freemason Grand Lodge in England and secured their own warrant to establish an African-American lodge. Over the years, the number of Masonic lodges dedicated to black Americans flourished. They still exist today and the order is called Prince Hall Masonry."

"Here's where the possibility that Freemasonry was the origin of the Poro and Sande gets interesting. Mind you, nothing conclusive but interesting nonetheless. Only a few decades later, the back-to-Africa movement began in earnest. Thousands of ex-slaves and freeborn blacks emigrated to Liberia and Sierra Leone. As you know, the abolitionists and their supporters facilitated the movement of them to this so-called land of freedom and opportunity. Needless to say, the many Americans who believed that blacks were subhuman creatures applauded the idea."

"I always wondered if there weren't some Freemasons aboard those ships that brought my people to the promise land, their ancestral home called Africa. It's just a thought given the similarities between the Freemasons and the Poro and Sande societies."

"I still don't see where you're going with this slice of history other than to establish that secret societies exist in Africa. Mary, other than catharsis what's your bottom line?"

"My bottom line as you say is that I'm Sande or a Sande, if you prefer. I was inducted into the society in my early teens and assigned an older mentor to teach me about the organization's mission and my place and purpose therein. I can't share its rituals but it does have many. Through subtle gestures and signs, I can readily recognize another Sande. It's not that I expect to instantly self-immolate if I disclosed them to you. It's more a matter of keeping the faith. I'm still a full-fledged member of Sande, not a dues-paying member, but a member nonetheless. One doesn't quit the Sande. Once a member, you're always a member unless you're kicked out for some indiscretion, such as revealing its secrets. Avery, you have *no need to know,* as we feds like to say. If you wish, you can Google both societies on the internet but you'll find little about them."

"But there's one thing you have to know about the Sande. All of its women have been circumcised. That's a prerequisite for membership and that's why my father did what he did. I had been chosen to serve and the ritual had to be performed as it had been from time immemorial. That's why I mentioned it so you would better understand the significance of the cultural mores and my allegiance to the society's rules and principles. That's an important secret and I shouldn't have told you. I may be damned by the gods for what I just revealed!"

"About the same time I was being tutored in the ways of the Sande, something else happened that would change my life forever. Charles Taylor's forces had occupied Grand Bassa County. He owned most of Liberia at that point. His men actively recruited more soldiers for his cause and many were children. I would become one of them. *Recruited* isn't the right word for what happened to me and others. I was conscripted, dragooned into Taylor's rebel army. My options were severely limited because I had none given the circumstances. If I had refused to serve, my parents and brother would have been killed."

"I was very lucky in one respect. Because of my age and good looks (or so I was told), I was assigned as a messenger, a courier. I didn't have to carry a rifle only pieces of paper; orders from Taylor's commanders to their subordinates inside Monrovia. I was taught to cut up the orders into small pieces, roll them up and coat them with coconut oil and shove them up my rectum for safekeeping."

"I made several successful crossings between Greater Monrovia and Monrovia. We were told to flirt with the security guards manning the check points to the city, not too much though. Invariably, they teased us and accused us of being spies for Taylor. It was all harmless banter between young, bored soldiers and a cutesy Mata Hari, at least until one day."

"That day I was questioned by a drunken government sentry who didn't have any interest in flirting. He accused me of being a spy and he wasn't joking. He dragged me about a hundred yards into the tall bush while his comrades-in-arms laughed. I knew what was about to happen. I was to be body cavity searched by his fingers and penis. He was interested in money and some pussy, a twofer. Women would often hide money in their snatches. The soldiers knew the trick and often used it as an excuse to finger probe those girls considered putative spies or who caught their eye. That's why we were instructed to hide our documents in our rectums. The soldiers were much less inclined to search there."

"I wasn't going to let a drunken boy not much older than me brutally rape me in the rainforest. More importantly, I couldn't let him find my secreted document. That would have meant instant death. When we arrived at a spot of his choosing, he immediately threw me to the ground and hovered over me on all fours. He was so close that I could smell the alcohol on his filthy breath. As he started pulling up my dress, I quickly removed the single-edged razor blade from my bra. I then reached up and slashed his throat from ear-to-ear. Blood gushed from his wound but he didn't say a word; couldn't say a word. He also had an involuntary bowel movement at that most inopportune time. Luckily, he was wearing a pair of dungarees so I didn't have any of his shit on me, only copious amounts of warm blood. I'll never forget the sight and smell. Those things still haunt my memories and dreams."

"That was the event that led me and my family to America. It was time to leave Liberia, posthaste, stat or ASAP, whichever one was quickest."

"I worked my way back home by travelling only at night. I couldn't be seen wearing a blood-soaked dress. That would raise too many eyebrows and questions. I told my parents what had happened and we all agreed it was time to leave the country. I wasn't the only one to be wanted by the authorities. My parents were equally at risk of premature death if the government troops captured them. We didn't know or care which side might ultimately win the war but we weren't willing to wait for the outcome. It was time to leave."

"We bribed a truck driver hauling a load of sugarcane to take us across the border to the Ivory Coast. We gave him enough money to bribe the border guards. The cane became our hiding place for the next 18 hours or so until we were safely inside the Ivory Coast. It wasn't a pleasant experience because the caning really hurt our backsides. It didn't take long for the local authorities to round us up and place us in a refugee camp on the outskirts of Abidjan. Actually, we were happy because we had little money and no food left."

"Like the other refugees, we waited our turn to be resettled in Europe or America. By the luck of the draw, we ended-up being resettled in Minnesota like many other Liberians before us. The rest is history as they say."

"Avery, I was all of thirteen years old when I killed that boy. Intellectually, I understand I had no choice. But emotionally I still suffer for what I did many years ago. I'm terribly ashamed about that. I have a strong moral compass, maybe too strong, but it's not pointing in the right direction in this case. Therapy has helped a little but I'm still emotionally conflicted and depressed over the incident. No, *the murder* is more accurate."

Mary started crying again but this time I didn't try to console her. She needed some space and privacy to let the tears flow. She'd feel better afterwards. However, it appeared that I wouldn't. I was afraid my aching ardors weren't about to be satisfied tonight.

Sometimes those who protect and serve desired someone to gently stroke their overactive libidos and aching privates, regardless of rankness.

Mary returned from the bathroom after about twenty minutes telling me it was time to finish her story, the part about Booku. I noticed she had freshened-up her makeup during her absence. Makeup or no makeup, she was a gorgeous woman. Jeez, I was starting to get a second wind!

"Thanks for putting up with my life story. The next part will only take a few minutes to relate. Hang-in there Avery and don't nod-off just yet. I think you'll really enjoy this part of the program."

"No problem. I've been thoroughly stimulated by the experience. What's next on the agenda?"

"This is the part where we hoist Merci Beaucoup on his very own petard. Literally speaking, that means we're going to blow him up with his own bomb."

That was an especially condescending remark by Mary. I was a bit miffed as we said in DS when we were really pissed-off about something. I knew she had graduated from Smith College with high honors but so what? I attended a state university that spoke English too, sort of. *Petard* was a smarmy French word though, what gives Ms. Know-it-all?

"So are we going to have someone place a bomb under his bed?" I explosively asked.

"No Avery, I was using a metaphor to explain..........."

"Stop it Mary! I understand what you're saying. I'm not totally stupid you know," I defensively and petulantly spoke. Perhaps I was somewhat stupid but not totally.

In any event, she didn't bother to confirm that I wasn't totally stupid and continued without so much as a *howdy do* or Howdy Doody. Regardless, I had my own Westernized vocabulary to defend against the Liberian wordplay she was using to impress me. Okay, bring it on bitch!

"Sorry Avery, but I was just trying to explain that we can use Booku's beliefs against him. I didn't mean to hurt your feelings or challenge the little boy hiding beneath your generous paunch."

I was getting angrier at Mary's newly found flippancy. I hadn't seen this side of her personality before and it was nasty. Maybe she was bipolar or manic-depressive. No, maybe she suffered from a multiple personality disorder. If so, I didn't like the one that had just emerged from her subconscious one bit.

Hold on a minute Avery, my twisted mind spoke. *What if there's a nymphomaniac slut with low self-esteem lurking about her cranium? Don't be too quick to judge the foibles of others, my friend. Play your cards right and you may score after all. Just don't be so damn impatient! Also, don't be too hard on yourself either for both our sakes. I'm starting to get a migraine listening to all of your fucking whining.*

Then again, maybe Mary and I were both stressed out. Maybe vigorous vaginal penetration was in order after all. I wasn't certain but I was ready to put on the gloves or condoms at this point. I only hoped for Mary's sake that I didn't mix-up the two. But given her pathology, I concluded that she probably wasn't too fond of men. Of that much, I was certain. I now believed that my fantasies and desires were down for the final count in this one-sided sparring match between the sexes. So, I finally threw in the towel and hopes in abject defeat. Enough was enough!

God, I hated quitters, even those who sometimes protect and serve for the good of our nation.

"What are you saying," I evenly asked while still seething from her earlier jibes and jabs.

"I'm saying that we go after Booku where he's most vulnerable—

his unswerving belief in the power of African magic. That's what I've been trying to tell you."

"Booku believes in the juju, the magic and the personal manifest destinies that go along with those unshakable beliefs. Despite or maybe because of his sociopathic personality, he's a true believer. What if we turn the tables on him and use the magic against him? I think that may totally undermine his self-confidence and destroy his sense of invincibility. The bigger they are, the harder they fall. Isn't that the American expression?"

I wasn't sure. Maybe Mary was testing my acumen in the English language again. No matter, I was starting to get excited by her strong logic and bold tactic to take Booku down. It was actually a brilliant idea but I didn't say so. I'd wait to see if it worked. If it did, I get some kudos along with Mary. If it didn't, Mary would twist alone in the wind. *Hoisted on her petard,* I think the expression goes. That was how things worked in DS too. You either were in the loop or outside of it. There was no middle ground these days. One had to choose carefully where they wanted to be in the muddled mix. However, it was mostly a crapshoot that came down to dumb luck.

Sometimes those who protect and serve gambled against overwhelming odds for a favorable outcome to their investigations, careers and sexual appetites.

"Earth to Avery, are you still with me? You seem to be drifting off to never-never land, my friend. Do I still have your undivided attention? Good, let me finish."

"Your question would naturally be: how do we do this? How do we make it happen? I have an answer and that's what I've been holding back."

"To make the answer simple, I know a person who can set Booku on his ear. He's a very powerful figure in the Poro. He's a senior leader who is extremely influential with the society and the Sande in Liberia and beyond. He's a respected person who wields much power if he chooses to exercise it and he's someone to be reckoned with. Even Booku will shake in his boots at the mere mention of his name. He's an authority figure beyond reproach. The Poro and Sande will follow his edicts without question if he decides to act. That's how much clout he exerts in Liberia. His word is law among the initiated and witting and therefore has tremendous influence over many thousands of believers. And here's the kicker—he's also the chief fetish priest for the Poro in Liberia. If we can enlist his support, we'll have Booku reeling from the body blow Fred can deliver. It's as straight forward and simple as that. This is doable. Please believe me."

"His name is Fred Tambo, my uncle and my father's blood brother. Please do not mention his name to anyone. I've told you too much already."

"Avery we need to pay Fred a visit and discuss what we have in mind for Booku. Fred's not enamored with Booku in the slightest. I know he wants democracy to flourish in Liberia. That's totally consistent with Poro beliefs and values."

"Avery, put on your best safari suit because we're leaving the day after tomorrow to visit Uncle Fred. That will give me enough time to talk to my father and convince him that he should talk to his brother about our plans. My father still feels guilty for what he did to me as a child so he'll go along with our plan for Booku's downfall. A guilty conscience serves as a great motivator as I've learned. Fred may be more difficult to convince but I think we can get him to support us. Given my light colored skin, he always believed I was a very special child sent by God for a noble purpose."

I didn't bother to correct Mary about my clothing. I was too exhausted to fight city hall or my colleague any longer. Okay, tomorrow I would buy a couple of dashiki shirts to satisfy my critics. *Did dashikis come with snap pockets?* I wondered. My Marlboros needed a home. Despite some misgivings, I reluctantly capitulated but without giving in. That's how we rationalized and parsed things in the department when we couldn't win an argument on merit.

Sometimes those who protcct and serve were much too tired to argue the more subtle nuances of haute couture or the utility of wearing finely-tailored leisure suits.

CHAPTER 13

UNCLE FRED STEPS UP TO THE PLATE

"Avery, the disinformation campaign's going well by all accounts," Frank mentioned as we stood in the MFA parking lot. "The people in Lofa County are abuzz with talk about Booku and the information we've been putting out to discredit him. Your idea of running scathing, humorous cartoons in the papers of Booku was very clever. You're humiliating him in the eyes of his followers. A lot of people, especially in the rural areas, can't read. But the messages are getting through to them as well—loud and clear. People are openly laughing about Booku and talking about what's going on."

"By the way, you had Her Nibs in stitches the other day with the cartoon showing the Booku character as each of the three monkeys seeing, speaking and hearing no evil. The fourth frame with Booku holding a skull with the caption of *doing no evil* was the crowning touch. The Oma was laughing so hard that tears ran down her face!"

"You need to understand something about us Liberians. Given

our political history, we are in awe of strong, aggressive leaders regardless of their viciousness and ruthlessness. It's a quirky thing but absolutely true. Conversely, we have no respect for weakness or for those that are perceived to be weak. We just can't stomach weaklings in any way, shape or form. Without doubt, Booku has been weakened by the all of the ridicule we've been throwing at him during the past week. Things are beginning to break our way."

"Frank, that's very interesting. It seems like our little psyche operation is working pretty well. Let's hope it'll result in some defections. We don't want to simply embarrass Booku, we want to undercut the support of his loyalists, the potential fighters. For the record, I didn't come up with the idea for the three monkey's piece. That was the brainchild of one of the editors you recruited. Those guys have great imaginations and know just the right buttons to push to exercise the readership. Frank, our radio spots start tomorrow. That should really increase the pressure on Booku. I only wish I knew his breaking point."

I wasn't so sure what mine was either.

"Frank, I've also told Mary to get with Lonestar to push out canned text messages questioning Booku's manhood. They will be something along the lines that only little boys and cowards hide in the jungle. If he had any balls, he would show himself."

Sometimes those who protect and serve were savvy media hounds who knew how to manipulate the system through pimps, pummels and a little monkey business.

Moses drove the old Camry straight and true but that wasn't what I wanted now. I told him to drive around the side streets for awhile to see if we were being tailed out of town. Uncle Fred had invited us to lunch at his place as Mary had hoped. I prayed that Fu-Fu wasn't on today's menu.

As we ensured our safety by slowly wending our way through the narrow streets of Monrovia, I noticed a woman poking at her head with a finger. That was odd and I told Moses to slow down even more so I could get a better look at what she was doing. As we approached, I saw the woman had a blotchy complexion that didn't correspond to the rest of her skin. I was puzzled and decided to venture a question with Ms. Know-it-all who was sitting next to me in the backseat.

"Mary, why does that woman keep poking her head?"

Mary laughed at my question but I didn't see what was so funny. I was getting tired of playing second fiddle to her purported intellectual superiority. Damn it! I could bang a drum with the best of percussionists.

"That's easy. She just came from the beauty shop where she had her plaits done. The knots are hurting her. She's poking at them to loosen them up a bit. That's the reason."

"Okay, but what about her blotchy face? Perhaps a cosmetology answer is in order?" I sarcastically asked.

"Well, well, you guessed right but the answer isn't so simple. She's bleached her face to lighten her skin color. She wants to be white or something closer to that state. In her case, whatever she used didn't work well."

"Why in the world would she do that to herself?"

"Perhaps it's a matter of self-loathing or low self-esteem or a belief that being white is somehow connected with being a better, maybe more godly, less evil person. Perhaps whiteness is simply a pop paradigm that is not-so-subtly conveyed in the movies and on TV. If your role models are attractive, successful white women, you want the same things for yourself. Forget the *black is beautiful* crap you've heard in the States. That's generally not true in Africa and elsewhere."

"Look, the phenomenon is not limited to this continent. Consider Asia and Latin America. Latinas with white, European blood are considered more attractive than native Indians or the mestizos. Even the women who work the rice paddies in Asia wear face coverings to keep the sun off. Sure, the practice is related to the heat but it's also a cultural thing so they don't darken their skin.

There it's even a religious thing, again the godliness aspect associated with light skin."

"Why do you think Booku is such a revered figure? It's not because he's a violent sociopath or rising political figure. There are a number of those people living in Liberia. No, the main reason is his unique skin color or lack of coloration in his case."

I mulled over what Mary had just related. What she said made sense but I wasn't going to admit that little piece of triviality to her. I was still smarting from her unkind remarks the other night.

Sometimes those who protect and serve were vain, passive-aggressive pouters who would like nothing better than to throw one hellacious temper tantrum.

According to Moses, our drive to Buchanan would take about three hours depending on road conditions. He mentioned that the Chinese had been repaving the road so we might make better time. Speaking of time, Mary and I passed ours by staring out of our respective windows and not talking to each other. It turned out to be a relaxing drive, especially for my damaged, exhausted ego.

We pulled into Buchanan shortly after noon. Mary had to ask around to find out where her uncle lived. It was an easy task since everyone knew. She hadn't seen her uncle in over 15 years and was nervous at the prospect of meeting him. Maybe it had something to do with our proposal or maybe it was something much more personal. I didn't know and didn't ask. Truthfully, I didn't have a bona fide *need to know*.

After Mary and her uncle embraced, I shook his hand and introduced myself. Fred Tambo was tall, just over six feet by my guesstimate. He was a commanding figure dressed in a plain white *agbada*, traditional West African garb usually reserved for special occasions. I suspected our visit fitted the bill.

"Mary, you've grown into a lovely woman!" Fred finally spoke. "I always believed you would, no doubt in my mind. But is your heart equally bright and beautiful? That's really what matters in this life, my child."

"Uncle, I've tried my best to follow the true ways that were taught to me as a teenager. However, I'm still troubled by things I've done in my past. But otherwise I've lived an honorable life. I've rigorously maintained the rituals and principles we both believe in."

"After we talk of the thing you came here for, we'll talk alone for awhile," Fred said. "We'll discuss the old ways of Mother Africa. Perhaps those things will relieve your pain and anguish over those past deeds that continue to bother you. You deserve to enjoy a life free from guilt and shame."

Maybe this guy could help break my nicotine addiction, I thought. *I had given up smoking many times but nothing seemed to work in the long run. Perhaps he'd prescribe some eye of newt or toe of frog. I'll skip the adder's fork and blind-worm's sting, thank you very much. I detested them even more than Fu-Fu.*

Sometimes those who protect and serve had trouble deciding on the efficacy of holistic healing and which doctor to choose.

Protocol called for sitting down to a meal before discussing business. We chatted about nothing in particular although discussed the changes in Buchanan since Mary and her family had left for the States. Frankly, that didn't take too long. Mary also reminisced about growing up in the small city, the friends she had made, the festivals she attended and the good times she had in her youth. It was all very moving, poignant and boring.

The forbidden words *Sande* and *Poro* were never once uttered during the meal. Our lunch consisted of grilled fish of one species or another that was covered in a brown sauce of one species or another. It had the consistency and color of grandma's gravy at Sunday dinner. It actually tasted pretty good but I didn't want to know what was in it. Bananas and coconut pieces rounded things out as dessert. Throughout lunch, Coca Cola was the drink de jour.

It was warm but I didn't mind too much. I actually enjoyed the meal although I had spilled some brown sauce on my new dashiki. I was terribly chagrined by my faux pas. I think that meant I had committed a clumsy mistake but I'd have to first check with Mary. Although I had been around guns my whole life, I was getting a little shy in my old age.

However, it was now time to palaver. The word as used in Africa didn't refer to idle chit-chat. It meant something much older and more meaningful. The early colonial explorers used the word to describe serious discussions and often negotiations with the natives. That meaning held true to this day. Palavering was part of every tribal meeting, major deliberation, social gathering and other situation of any consequence. A palaver was akin to a powwow in the Amerindian tradition but without the smoky bonfires that caused your eyes and nose to water.

Mary was our designated palaverer. She had more experience than I did in this particular parlance. I'd keep quiet unless I accidentally belched or farted. But I didn't plan to do either. This discussion was much too important to interrupt or screw-up. Mary knew which of her uncle's buttons to push and when. I'd stay mum and silent too. I'd also keep my fingers crossed behind my back for good luck. I figured that every little advantage helped during a critical palaver between blood relatives. Moreover, I didn't have the slightest idea what we were doing talking to a powerful witch-doctor. I'd have to suspend my credulity and skepticism at least until we got home. I'd then down a couple of glasses of Zinfandel to restore my confidence in good, old-fashion Western-style logic and a fine California vintage.

"Uncle Fred, you know why we have come to you. Father has explained much already but I wanted to discuss this thing in person so you could see what's in my heart. I also badly needed to see my favorite uncle after so many years apart. I've often thought of you fondly over the past many years. I've missed you so much!" Mary even shed a couple of tears for dramatic effect to seal the deal. God, she was a great little actress. I greatly admired her chutzpah and finely-curved ass.

Not only was Mary bright, she knew how to suck-up to the old man. Unfortunately, I'd never be on the receiving-end of her cloyed mouthing. I had a strong gut feeling below my paunch about that immutable fact.

"Merci Beaucoup is a scourge, blight on our country. He has been responsible for much misery among our people over the years. He has spilled innocent blood for personal and political reasons. His viciousness is well known throughout our land. People fear him yet he has many supporters from the Taylor days. You know these things to be true."

The three of us were sitting in the shape of a triangle on the concrete floor of Fred's hut. I didn't know if palavering required some sort of seating pattern or not. I'd simply sat down when the others did. Maybe we were now closer to Mother Africa and empowered to learn her secrets. I hoped she didn't make an appearance because that apparition would have scared the beejesus out of me. I was having enough difficulty holding my own wind. I gently rocked back-and-forth on my cheeks to stifle a fart that was building up inside me. Perhaps I wouldn't be able to keep my mouth shut after all.

Without responding to Mary, Fred turned to me. "Mr. Dick you should not be present when we discuss such matters. However, I've made an exception out of deference and love for my niece. I expect you will not betray my trust. You must never discuss what is said or seen today with anyone other than Mary. If you do, you will suffer unpleasant consequences. Do you understand my meaning?"

I nodded my head indicating that I'd gotten the threat.

"Good, yes I know Booku and his evil ways as well. Many Liberians have suffered at his hand. Our brotherhood has always tried to stay away from politics and government institutions. We believe we are above such petty things and answer to a higher authority. Our apolitical stance has worked well in the past and I'm reluctant to change the order of things. Why should I Mary? Why is this matter so important?"

"It's important to our people uncle. It's important to avoid bloodshed and it's important to bring peace and stability to Liberia. What you don't know is that Booku is planning to overthrow the Sirleaf government by force. He's been actively recruiting soldiers and will soon begin their training in bush camps he's established in Lofa County. We both know that Ellen Sirleaf will not leave office without a fight. It's not in the Iron Lady's nature. She's gone into exile once but won't again given her age and determination to bring democracy to our nation. She'll defend Liberia with all the resources at her disposal. Those resources are scant at the moment and I believe Booku's forces will have the upper-hand in any battle scenario."

"You know what that will mean for our people—terror, deprivation, suffering and many injuries and deaths among the innocent. It will be like the wars years but I believe much worse because of the lopsided number of trained combatants. Booku has the advantage at the moment although we've been undermining his plans. As best we can tell, they're working and his position and stature has been weakened as a result. However, he's still a formidable figure and serious threat to President Sirleaf."

"We can't allow Booku to succeed. The consequences are too horrible to even think about. That's why you must act, dear uncle. You must issue a taboo!"

Mary explained the difference between a taboo and a curse during the drive home. I was positive they were spelled differently but that was about all. Apparently, I still had much to learn about Africa. Basically, I learned that a taboo was a prohibition against something; a curse was sort of a spell with its bad connotations directed against a specific recipient. The Poro and Sande never issued curses, only taboos. Curses posed a bit of a dilemma for the curser. In popular lore, what was avowed would return to the curser tenfold. They had a boomerang effect and you had to be damn careful in uttering them. However, I didn't personally believe a word of this voodoo, hoodoo, juju crap although I vowed to swear less in the future. But I'd always wanted one of those cool, pink rabbit's feet for my keychain. It didn't hurt to periodically hedge one's bets for positive karma.

"Mary, you've made a good case for issuing a taboo that would prohibit Booku and his followers from taking-up arms against President Sirleaf. Booku will likely laugh it off but his people won't, even those who do not share our beliefs. None will dare to break it and risk retribution from the ancient gods."

"What you have said rings true to my ears. Bringing peace and prosperity back to our country is wholly consistent with our values and beliefs. I believe the gods would favor a taboo under these circumstances. It would avoid more civil strife and misery. I agree to the taboo."

With that, Fred closed his eyes and went into a trance, maybe he was on a vision quest too. Then again, he might just be sleeping-off the big lunch we had just finished. I couldn't be sure. But I expected more than just some snoozing during this exercise or exorcise.

I waited for the native dancers wearing hula skirts to enter his hut and start dancing around to the beating of loud drums. I had a hunch they'd have fearsome symbols painted all over their bodies and bones in their noses. It didn't happen. Actually, nothing happened, other than Fred continuing his nap. I even scanned the small room to discover any evidence of witchery. However, I saw nothing noxious or vile unless you counted the tin of Folgers instant coffee sitting on a shelf.

Sometimes those who protect and serve were badly misinformed about African customs and traditions by watching too many Tarzan movies and coffee commercials starring Mrs. Olson while growing up.

Fred finally awoke from his trance and quietly spoke only two words: *it's done.* Okay, one was actually a contraction but I didn't think it made any difference to the ancient, wise ones he'd just spoken to.

Mary told me to get lost and wait outside. She was actually more polite but I didn't want to give her any quarter in our little tiff. Regardless, my constant snuffling and sniveling were getting annoying for both of us. Hell's bells, I also realized that I didn't get a chance to ask Fred about my smoking problem!

I found a large tree to sit under while I chain-smoked waiting for Mary to finish with her uncle. I pondered what had just transpired. Fred had issued a taboo that would prevent most natives from fighting for Booku. Without fighters, Booku was dead in the water so to speak. I liked the *dead* part. The word had a nice ring to it especially when applied to a monstrous ghoul such as Monsieur Merci Beaucoup. Half of our mission appeared to have been accomplished but capturing Booku was the cherry on the icing on the cake. It was obvious that we had more work to do in Hell's kitchen, I meant Liberia.

Then it hit me—squarely on the head! How could I have missed it? I wasn't discovering the laws of gravity but rather being attacked by an almond fruit that had fallen from above. Of all of the trees in Africa, I had chosen to sit under my nemesis, nightly companion and ersatz bottle of *No Doze*—an obnoxious, frigging almond tree. I quickly concluded that there really wasn't any rest for the wicked or stupid of this world. But I was at least smart enough to move to a less fruitful species nearby. Maybe the African gods had forsaken me.

Mary finally emerged from her uncle's shanty. I noticed she was wearing a necklace that I hadn't seen before, perhaps a gift from her uncle. Then it dawned on me; it wasn't just a necklace, it was an amulet to protect her from harm. Uncle Fred was taking no chances in protecting his favorite niece.

We rounded up Moses who had been kibitzing with the neighbors for the past several hours. Maybe he was palavering with them too. In any case, we hit the road and hoped to be back in Monrovia before nightfall. As dangerous as the roads were during the day, they were downright suicidal at night. People, animals and debris of all description littered the roadways of Liberia. Add the inexperienced and often drunk drivers to the mix and you got some sense of the risk and the odds of retaining our mortality. Unlike many countries, there were few roadside chapels (called a *park and pray* in Liberia) to increase one's chances of survival. Therefore, Moses would get stuck playing the role of St. Christopher. He would be my very own talisman and lucky charm. Two could play the gods too!

Mary was noticeably relaxed and calm after talking to her uncle. I hoped she had shed some of her angst and bitchiness through his ministrations. However, her menstruations might still pose a problem in terms of her equanimity. However, I didn't plan to stay around her long enough to find out.

"Thanks Avery for your moral support and silence while Uncle Fred deliberated over his decision to help us. He was very nervous and uncomfortable with you being there. But I think he appreciated your respectfulness. That sort of demeanor helped our argument greatly."

Maybe things were beginning to thaw between Mary and me. I believed that was the first compliment she had paid me. If she wanted to patch things up, I was certainly willing to meet her a quarter of the way. I could be especially magnanimous when situations and my arrogance dictated.

"Avery, I'm not trying to irritate you, but why have you been rubbing your scalp for the past fifteen minutes? I'm just curious."

I told her I was only loosening my plaits that were hurting. Mary immediately shot me a knowing glance as in *I know you're a fucking dick, Avery. Don't deny it asshole!*

Sometimes those who protect and serve were more than willing to smoke the peace pipe or viscerally bury the hatchet with their adversaries.

We'd been travelling a couple of hours and it was starting to get dark. We still had another hour to go before we reached Monrovia. Night in Africa was a special time and place. Without the haze of pollution, the stars shone clear and bright overhead. You could easily see the many constellations in the Southern Hemisphere with the naked eye. An inexpensive telescope would bring them even closer. I thought our stars were finally aligning too. I felt good about we had accomplished so far and, despite my earlier pique, I acknowledged that Mary had done a fantastic job all the way around. If I could tell the whole truth and nothing but, I'd say she was more useful than I in bringing our investigation and disinformation campaign forward. Of course, I could never do that given my strict DS upbringing.

My stargazing and reverie were interrupted by Moses telling us he had to stop to take a leak. We both knew that gas stations and 7-11s were in short supply in Liberia so impromptu pit stops were common. He turned off the headlights and switched off the ignition. I didn't pay him much mind since Mary and I were engaged in a friendly conversation about African history. She had honorably delivered on her three-fourths of the reconciliation. We were buds again!

Much to our shock the car started to move forward of its own accord or so we thought at the time. Our shock included the fact that it was a Toyota and not a Honda. Damn it, Moses had forgotten to set the handbrake! I quickly glanced between the bucket seats and immediately noticed that Moses had also left the gearshift in neutral. I'd give him a royal ass-chewing and high colonic for his carelessness when he got back. With his experience, he should have known better. I quickly determined that he did know what he was doing. But it wasn't a nice or Christian gesture.

I spun my head around and saw two figures pushing our car forward. Before I could get my Glock out of my trousers or otherwise react, our car headed down a steep embankment, ending up in a body of water. Of that much I could be sure given the large amount of the stuff pouring through Moses' side window, the one he had thoughtfully left open. We were both thrown forward despite wearing seatbelts. I suffered some abrasions to my face, maybe my nose was broken too, but Mary was moaning in pain. I was terribly worried about her condition.

I unbuckled both of us and waited for the water to fill the car. Given the pressures, I knew I couldn't open a door until they had equalized. Mary was going in-and-out of consciousness and I didn't have much time to get us out of the car and our predicament. As the water approached the ceiling of the car, I pulled the handle and used my legs to push the door open. It was difficult but it worked. We were now free from the vehicle and a watery grave. I dragged Mary behind me until we reached the surface. The water wasn't that deep but the surface current was ferocious. I had a hard time holding onto Mary and keeping my own head above water.

It was now pitch black and I was terribly disoriented in what I believed to be a fast-moving river. I could barely make out shapes before me. At one point, I reached out in desperation and luckily snagged a large tree branch jutting into the river. If I hadn't, I wasn't sure how much longer I could have held onto Mary or myself. She was now limp and quiet in my arms. Those weren't good signs and I suspected she'd been seriously injured when we hit the water.

I managed to move both of us along the branch until I could stand without being swept away by the currents. I gently lifted Mary to the muddy bank and sat for a few seconds to regain my strength and wits. As I did, I was grabbed by my hair from behind and brusquely pulled a few feet up the embankment. I was screaming in pain but my attacker was silent. He showed no mercy whatsoever for my plight. That was because he was one of Merci's goons, a coldblooded and heartless killer. It was time for my comeuppance and demise. I understood what was in store for me and Mary and it wasn't good.

I fumbled for my Glock in my soaked pants but it was missing. I must have lost it in the river. By instinct and a strong rush of adrenaline, I twisted my body a 180 degrees and grabbed my attacker's ankles. My hair must have ached but it didn't make any difference because I didn't feel a thing. He fell backwards to the ground and released his grip while doing so. I immediately pounced on him and punched him once in the face to get his attention. He bled from his lips but didn't stop struggling. It seemed he needed another, more pointed lesson in DS-style civility.

I quickly removed my belt buckle knife from its concealed sheath sewn into my wide leather belt. I gripped its rectangular handle and pushed the four inch blade into the stomach of my would-be assassin. With both hands, I pulled it upwards to his sternum, piercing his pericardium in the process. His body immediately stopped moving. I could see from his glazed eyes and thousand yard stare that I had mortally wounded him. He would bleed-out in less than a New York minute. To my clouded mind, he looked like death warmed over. I then rolled his body down the slope and into the water. With any luck, it would end up in Lofa County. Accidental drowning was not that uncommon in Liberia.

Sometimes those who protect and serve played hardball with those fanatics who challenged the will of Uncle Sam and his loyal minions.

I next turned my thoughts and attentions to Mary. I scooted down the embankment and went to her aid. As I reached the waterline, I looked around but couldn't find her! I started to panic again. Maybe she had been swept downriver by the strong currents so I frantically searched for her along the bank. I even called out her name several times but to no avail. She was gone.

I sat down. I was totally wiped-out from the ordeal we had just experienced. But out of the corner of my eye I noticed something in the shallow water about ten yards from where I was sitting. As I approached the object, I could see it was Mary's partially submerged body. I pulled her to shore and checked for vital signs. I detected a sketchy pulse and very slow, shallow breathing. She wasn't conscious, maybe that was a blessing under the circumstances. But thank God she was still alive!

With the little strength I had left, I carried Mary up the slope and to the road. Her body was now shaking from shock. I had to get her medical help soon or she would die. I looked to the night sky and swore she wouldn't die in my arms. I'd drop the bitch like a hot potato before that happened!

I flagged down the first car that came along. The driver must have been surprised at the sight. He stopped and immediately understood that we had been involved in some sort of road mishap. Seeing Mary's condition, he ran to the bush and cut several large palm fronds and covered her body to keep her warm. With little conversation, he drove us to the Firestone Hospital located about 15 miles away.

I learned later that Mary was one lucky person. There were only two hospitals up to U.S. standards in the entire country. One was Firestone, the other was the United Nations Jordanian Medical Unit located on the far side of Monrovia. All of the other hospitals in Liberia were little more than morgues-in-waiting. Mary's uncle must have been working overtime on behalf of his beloved niece. I'd no longer question the power of African magic.

The doctors later told me that Mary had suffered a collapsed lung and several broken ribs in addition to some superficial cuts and abrasions to her face. Most importantly, they said she would pull through but would spend several days in the hospital recovering from her injuries. That was great news! My broken nose was set and I was free to go home but I refused. Instead, I'd stay at the hospital and watch over Mary. She was now conscious but groggy from the sedatives she'd been given for her pain. Okay, now I could easily win any wordplay arguments with her for a change. So much for those highfalutin Smith College educations!

I borrowed a cell phone and called Frank. I related what had happened to us. He was glad to hear that Mary was doing okay but absolutely furious to learn that Moses Kekula had betrayed us. He cryptically commented that he knew where Moses lived. He didn't elaborate and I didn't question him. In any event, I suspected that Moses Kekula would get his just reward, probably in heaven, sooner or later. I was now impatient so I mentally voted for sooner.

In all of the commotion, I'd forgotten about our Good Samaritan! When I realized my inconsiderate behavior, I rushed to the main entrance to the hospital where he had dropped us off. He was nowhere to be found. I hadn't even bothered to ask his name. Hopefully, in his case, his good deed would be recognized in heaven or wherever he ended up in the afterlife. I felt like a piece of shit for not being able to thank him.

While sitting at Mary's bedside, I decided to strike the word *alive* from Booku's wanted posters. That option was no longer open to him now. I vowed, but didn't curse, that I would find the son-of-a-bitch and kill him with my own hands. I'd leave Moses' fate to Frank and God. With all of the bribe money, I meant stipend, Moses still clung to his old ways and former masters. Steadfastness and loyalty were admirable traits in most situations. Regardless, I'd just found my first principled man in Liberia. Maybe that counted for something.

Sometimes those who protect and serve left no stone unturned and took nothing for granite when tracking down their quarry.

CHAPTER 14

BEAT OF DIFFERENT DRUMMERS

The best defense is a good offense or so they say. I could never figure out who *they* were and I guessed I'd never know. But that was the tact I would take with Phil Jensen. I'd never had any problem being offensive before so I thought I could keep him on the defensive while I explained my little mishap. It certainly wouldn't be the truth, but a reasonable approximation thereof. That meant I'd be lying through my teeth again. By the way, I now had one less to worry about.

I did a quick knock on his office door and marched in. He was alone and sitting with his back to me. When he turned around, he began laughing, not little tee-hees or even a weak guffaw but a hearty, full-fledged belly laugh. I just couldn't stomach those.

When he stopped his humiliating behavior, he asked what had happened to my nose.

"Run into that proverbial door, Avery? Did your lady friend's irate husband discover you poking your nose in places where it didn't belong? Jeez, you look like Jimmy Durante on steroids!"

My planned march to the sea had just been cut short. Phil had seized the initiative and day and was keeping me on the defensive with his banter. My plan had not worked to plan.

"Yuck it up Phil but I'm in pain. It wasn't the women this time but the booze. I drank too much wine last night and slipped on the bathroom floor and went face first into the commode. Look, I even lost a tooth."

I pulled one check back to reveal the gap. "Also, don't you say a fucking word about my accident with a Liberian loo. I have enough baggage already to carry around and I don't need any more."

"Sure, no problem buddy, your secret's safe with me brother," as he began laughing again. "Just remember the DS motto: *what's a secret if you can't tell a friend!*"

I felt relieved knowing my secret would be safe with Phil, at least until the next person walked through the door. It must have been a male bonding thing between kindred spirits.

"Okay, okay asshole, I'm not here looking for sympathy or your putdowns. Moses, my driver, has gone missing. He hasn't shown up for work in the past two days and that's crimping my style." I was trying to gin up some righteous indignation but it wasn't working. Phil had effectively trumped my little ploy.

"That's not all that unusual here. Family emergencies come up and employees take off for a few days. The only thing surprising is that he didn't get word to you. I'll arrange for another driver until he gets back. I don't want to be accused of holding up your important work here. How's it going by the way?"

"Great, just great Phil, I'm absolutely impressed with what you and the advisors have accomplished in your short time in Liberia. My report will reflect that fact. The numbers all jibe and the books are well-maintained. There's no way the Hill can question the expenditures of Uncle Sam's monies. Phil, you and your team are to be commended!"

Phil beamed while soaking-up my bullshit. He'd remember the lie when he found out there would be no report, no program review and no accolades. He'd be righteously pissed and wouldn't forgive me for my pimping. Too bad, I thought it would be a good object lesson in camaraderie and male bonding.

I decided it wasn't a good time to mention my missing Glock. Even Phil's credulousness had limits. Besides, I couldn't think of a good or wholly plausible lie, I meant explanation, at the moment.

"Have a better day, Big Bird," Phil laughingly said as I left his office. I took his laughter in stride as I walked to the lift knowing that I'd get the last one.

Sometimes those who protect and serve grimly spun bullshit into gold for the naïve and gullible of the kingdom.

I visited Mary at home where she was recuperating from her traffic accident. Reportedly, she was riding in the backseat of a taxi when it was struck by another car at an intersection on Bushrod Island. At least that was what she told her boss and coworkers. Her boss wished her a speedy recovery and admonished her for using the local taxis. They were off-limits for UN staff and most embassy personnel due to safety concerns. In this instance, compassion didn't neatly mesh with bureaucratic edicts.

She said she was feeling much better but still experiencing a lot of pain. I told her to drink a couple glasses of wine, take a Percocet and she'd be feeling good in no time. I wasn't worried about our OPSEC practices any longer since Booku knew all, thanks to Moses Kekula. Mary lived on the main UN compound that was well protected. I didn't worry about her safety while she remained home. That appeared to be just what the doctor ordered. She'd be bedridden for another week and then allowed to resume duties at work on a part-time basis only.

Mary mentioned that she'd spoken to her uncle Fred about the incident. He said he'd already heard and was furious with Booku for the attempt on her life. That might motivate him to taboo even harder. Moreover, he probably learned of our skirmish in the bush via jungle drums or a late night vision. More likely, he heard it through old fashion gossip or palavering as the case might be.

Mary would be out of commission for awhile so I needed Frank's help to finish our assignment. The assignment had changed recently. It now included assassinating Mr. Booku with very extreme prejudice. Frank had been watching my behind for several weeks and I was getting tired of being treated as a sex object. I was beginning to feel cheap and dirty from his furtive glances. I even got paranoid every time I bent over to tie my wingtips knowing he was watching my backside. No more, it was time for Frank to give up his bodyguard duties and take a more prominent role in our mission. I needed someone to buttress and sustain our disinformation campaign and I couldn't think of a more qualified person for the job. *Ecce homo!* That guy was none other than Frank Yeaten.

One thing that bothered all of us was the fact that Moses could have killed Mary and me with a couple of well-placed bullets to our heads with no muss or fuss. Why did Booku order him to stage an accident? Our first guess made sense. Moses didn't want to be associated with an obvious crime. He would tell the truth, sort of anyway. He'd say he had to stop to take a leak and had forgotten to set the handbrake. He felt badly about what had happened but it was simply a tragic accident. That would sell with the authorities since ignorance and stupidity weren't criminal offenses. That was because there weren't enough jail cells in Liberia to hold the many offenders.

An equally good explanation was that Booku didn't want to create any martyrs. Our public relations plan was working well. He was gradually being pulled out of hiding and would have to show his people that he was still a powerful force. His people had always viewed him as a strong, commanding, almost god-like figure. If he were so damn strong and powerful, why would he bother killing weak people of no consequence? Maybe, just maybe, he wasn't invincible after all? Maybe, just maybe, he was flawed and wholly human like the rest of the people? Maybe, just maybe, he wouldn't or couldn't be the supreme leader the people desired so much?

My guess was that Booku couldn't risk damaging his credibility at this juncture. He didn't deign to kill us in a manner that could be traced back to him. He couldn't afford any doubts about his leadership abilities either. Yes, an accident was God's will and not Booku's doing. That would fit nicely with his warped psyche and consistent with the mindsets of his followers. He stubbornly refused to stoop to conquer.

Sometimes those who protect and serve ascribed crime theories with the flimsiest of evidence and most optimistic wishful thinking imaginable.

Frank was a little nervous when I told him he would be taking on additional duties as assigned. But I think he clearly understood the meaning of that artful statement. It meant that he would now be my butt-boy and carry the water for me. If he didn't like it, he could complain to the Oma. I believed he feared her more than Booku so he didn't bother to challenge me.

Speaking of the Oma, she was now juggling a political hot potato. Opposition newspapers were accusing her of interfering with the democratic processes and political freedoms of the people of Lofa County. The diatribes were couched in such a way as to avoid mentioning Booku's name but nonetheless were scathing attacks on Ellen Sirleaf's government. It seemed that Booku's friends were starting to push back. One paper, *The Voice of Liberty*, went so far as to claim that she personally was behind the disinformation campaign we had crafted and put into effect.

Local elections in Lofa were looming and her critics were making every effort to link the campaign to them. While President Sirleaf had more-or-less clean hands in terms of our operation, she still had to be careful not to alienate the people she governed. That would have been contrary to her twin goals of fostering unity and rebuilding the nation. Any serious schism among the populace could have spelled trouble for her and Liberia.

President Sirleaf was no fool. She understood the media game and knew how to play. She enlisted the help of some close friends to counteract the negative press she was receiving. One of her dearest buds was the U.S. embassy. It very quietly and discreetly let it be known that it was displeased with all of the vitriolic rhetoric being directed against the Oma and her government.

Keep the infighting above the belt children was the clear message it sent to the opposition leaders. *We're not trying to interfere in your country's internal affairs but you need to lower the volume so the neighbors don't complain. Oh, by the way, the funding for our educational scholarships and public diplomacy grants is really tight this year. Uncle Sam will have some tough decisions to make as to who gets those goodies. Do your relatives have any alternate plans for next year? I also forgot to mention that multiple-entry visas to the States might be a wee bit tight too. Jeez, terrorism really put a damper on the numbers. How's your son doing at Penn State these days? Have a good one, my friend!*

American diplomacy had again won the battle for hearts and minds. The Oma's political opponents turned down the heat and the print press returned to its normal pap of reporting vehicle accidents, weddings, crimes and gross misspellings of words.

Sometimes those who didn't protect and serve recognized that America welcomed its friends with open arms, greased palms and clenched fists.

CHAPTER 15

STYX AND STONES

"Avery, don't you dare say it! I know your quirky mind and its hidden prejudices. It's not the least bit funny," Mary angrily spoke from her sickbed.

I was paying Mary another daily visit to check on her condition, pep her up and lend her my moral support. Apparently, I wasn't being successful with the latter goal because I didn't have any morals at my age. I'd simply asked her how her uncle was going to communicate his taboo throughout Liberia. I didn't know if under juju rules such things could be conveyed by telephone or letter or whatever. It was *whatever* that was now bothering Mary. It was Mary's claimed ability to read my mind that was bothering me. It appeared I was in big trouble over my head again.

"No, he's not going to use jungle drums, you frigging jerk. I know that's what you're thinking. You can't fool me."

Whew, I was off the mental hook. Mary had badly misjudged what I was thinking. Actually, I thought Fred would use young boys holding long lianas and swinging from tree-to-tree to get his message across. I'd seen that technique on TV so it had to be true. Regardless, women could be so damn judgmental at times.

"He'll send out runners, I mean messengers, to each chief of each major tribe in the country. That's about fifty in all. There will be no written message only a memorized script that must be precisely spoken so there are no misunderstandings about its meaning. The chiefs will relay the taboo throughout their tribal lands to their kinsmen. About now, Merci Beaucoup should be feeling and seeing its effect. The scene will resemble Moses parting the sea. His supporters and those sitting on the political fence will part as well. The taboo is too powerful to be ignored."

Her reference to Moses and water made my stomach feel a little queasy. But I was able to stifle the bit of bile that was heading to my throat. It tasted like sweet revenge.

The hand printed note arrived just after I awoke the next morning. The gate guard at my compound had personally delivered it. I didn't bother to ask if he had precisely memorized it as well. Maybe Uncle Fred had thoughtfully dropped me a copy of his message. However, that wasn't the case.

The missive was from Booku and it read as follows:

We are at cross-purposes Mr. Dick and needn't be. We share the same ultimate, long-term goal—oil and natural gas. America badly needs the energy Liberia can provide in the near future. Our reserves are estimated to be many millions of barrels of high-grade oil and billions of cubic feet of gas. Billions of petrodollars are at stake. If you and your government agree to quietly back-away from your efforts to stop me from toppling Ellen Sirleaf's regime and seizing the presidency, you both will be well-rewarded. I will promise, in writing, to sell the United States 75% of Liberia's production at below market rates for a period of ten years. I won't renege on the bargain because you will have the letter of agreement I will sign. If that became public knowledge, it would be my death warrant. As for you personally, I offer an immediate commission of $50,000 for your services as an honest broker. That's double the amount you offered for me. More will be offered later for your continued cooperation.

We are both men of the world and should be able to rise above petty politics. Neither of us truly cares what happens to this country. The world bodies care even less. Liberia's just another backwater, African shithole to them. It has only one thing of any value—petroleum and lots of it. Let's put aside our differences and work together to make this deal happen. It's a win-win situation all the way around.

If you agree to my terms, meet me at the Marlin Corners dock at 9 pm tomorrow. Come alone and I will do the same. Do not worry about your safety. You have a very powerful ally in Fred Tambo and I will not act against you, as much as I'd like to.

Not surprisingly, the note wasn't signed but I had no doubt about the author's identity. I also had an overwhelming gut feeling that I should thoroughly wash my hands after reading it since *cleanliness was next to godliness.* "What a crock," as they often said in Liberian English!

Sometimes those who protect and serve were glad they'd met Evelyn Wood in their storied youths.

Frank read Booku's letter very slowly and I saw his lips wordlessly form some of the words. Obviously, his speech skills were more pronounced than his reading abilities.

"Booku's running scared," Frank declared. "I think he's serious about the offer and he wouldn't have cut such a deal unless his back was against the wall. Watch out Avery, he's still got some teeth left."

I instinctively put a finger in my mouth and rubbed my empty socket while my mind wandered. The 50 grand was a lot of tax-free money. I didn't think Booku would file a 1099 with the IRS so I'd be scot-free if I accepted it.

I'd already made up my mind to meet Booku and take the bribe. I was a bit miffed at the small amount he'd offered to sell-out my principles and country, but what the hell. It wasn't chump change by any means. In fact, the amount could sustain my boozing, whoring and smoking unfiltered cigarettes for many years to come. *There is a God after all,* I thought and I was feeling better already. Praise the

Lord and pass the visceral vices. I was finally heading to the promised land of tall cotton, milk and honey and sweet clover!

The combination of cash crops just didn't get any better in my book. However, I was terribly puzzled and worried about making hay while the sun still shined. I guessed that was my last straw and couldn't have everything. Regardless of drawing life's long or short one, I refused to bet the farm on any of this pastoral, agrarian crap.

"Frank, what's a Marlin Corners?" I was still having problems deciphering the local lingo.

Frank chuckled and said it was a bar and restaurant on the St. Paul River that was mostly patronized by expatriates. When he told me that, I thought I could fit right in with the crowd since I was an expatriate and often patronizing. Thankfully, I wouldn't need to wear a disguise.

Sometimes those who protect and serve closeted and costumed themselves when no one watched their backsides.

I had Frank drive me to Marlin Corners. It didn't take much convincing because he cringed slightly every time I mentioned the Oma's name. We arrived about a half hour early and I marked time by having a glass of Zinfandel at the bar. Frank bided his time by sitting in the car twiddling his thumbs and cracking his knuckles. I sincerely hoped arthritis didn't run in his family.

As I sipped the fine wine, I watched a bunch of obnoxious, sloppy drunks playing darts in the corner. They were loud and rude so I took them for American NGOs. Luckily, I was out of range so the darts pricks wouldn't pose a problem. But I still decided to find another spot to sit.

I moved myself and my drink to the veranda to be closer to the water and away from the sportsmen. The St. Paul was dark and calm but it gave off a nauseating stench from its pollution. Regrettably, I couldn't hold my nose.

I could see a few house lights on the far shore and one small light on the river itself. It was getting brighter which meant the boat was getting closer. *It must be my date,* I thought. I walked down to the dock and stood by. As the boat drew closer, I could see the light was a small flashlight attached to the bow. The single figure sitting in it was less recognizable given the distance.

I wondered what Booku looked like and, more importantly, what he would be wearing. I had heard the stories and now it was time to find out for myself. My pride and good fashion sense demanded nothing less than being dressed to the 9s for our meeting. No other odd number would do. I could be damn fussy at times and as circumstances suggested. Of course, *prissiness* was out of the question for a macho federal agent like me. That was why I dressed in black from head to toe so I could emulate the clothing worn by my nemesis. No one-upmanship here, only a level playing field for those about to go toe-to-toe. Speaking of which, my highly polished black wingtips glistened under the dock's lights. I gave them one last dusting-off by rubbing them on the backs of my pants legs. Too bad they might get dirty tonight by kicking some ghoulish ass.

Sometimes those who protect and serve enjoyed playing the role of the cat's meow rather than a run-of-the-mill pussy.

The 20 foot fishing boat puttered slowly to where I was standing. I could now clearly see Merci Beaucoup and terribly shocked by what I saw. Instead of wearing his trademark all-black clothes, he was dressed in a gold, hooded sweatshirt that had a superimposed photo of Cinderella's Castle at Disneyworld. I could make out Walt and Mickey holding hands in front of it. Moreover, he was sporting blue jeans and a pair of white Reebok sneakers. I was overdressed and thoroughly embarrassed—so much for Liberian intelligence. Jeez, couldn't these people get anything right?

I'd wasted a lot of time and some money foolishly primping for this event. I'd worn my black leisure suit with black, calf-length socks. Normally, I'd only don the suit for diplomatic receptions and similar soirees requiring semiformal attire. Proper grooming and clothes made the man in the Foreign Service. No matter, the garters were now pinching my flesh and slowly cutting off the circulation to my lower legs. I soon might not have a leg to stand-on when standing-up to Booku and defending America's honor. Not to be outdone in headgear, I'd also bought a handsome, black Panama hat. However, I had to remove the rainbow-colored ribbon from its crown because it clashed with my outfit. But here was a frumpily dressed Booku sitting in a rickety old boat on the odorous St. Paul River. What did that say about him? More to the point, what did it say about me? Luckily, I didn't get a chance to answer myself.

"Get in the boat Mr. Dick!" There were no formal introductions or exchange of normal and expected pleasantries. We didn't bother to shake hands but that was fine with me. But it was an inconsiderate and rude beginning to an acquaintanceship that might only last a couple of minutes if Booku decided to throw me to the nasty things lurking beneath the boat.

He hit the throttle and the boat sped away from the dock. I noticed two things about Booku that the gossip got right. His facial pallor was as white as a ghost that had just seen its own reflection. The second was the heavily tinted, wraparound sunglasses he was wearing. The intelligentsia had nailed that particular feature to a tee. I was relieved I couldn't see his eyes. I also prayed that he wouldn't remove his shades in my presence, flashing back on the earlier horror tales. I knew the eyes were the windows to the soul. As insightful as they might be, I still didn't want to peek into his.

He pointed the boat upriver and gunned the motor. I suspected we weren't going anyplace in particular but I wanted it to be a roundtrip excursion in any event. After travelling about a mile, he abruptly cut the engine and we gently floated with the current. It was another clear night and the stars shone brightly overhead. The moon was full and illuminated the river creating a glassy sheen. The night was simply beautiful and perhaps could've been described as romantic under different circumstances. But I still anxiously waited for Booku to propose. He finally did and I was thrilled. For what it was worth, I played hard to get at first, only later giving myself to him. However, I wasn't quite sure who would end-up on top in the relationship.

Sometimes those who protect and serve must coyly dissemble and play a female character to seduce and foil an antagonistic actor.

"Mr. Dick, you already have my proposal. I assume you've accepted its terms or you wouldn't be here. Am I correct?"

"I thought it was interesting and personally advantageous. $50,000 is a lot of money anywhere in the world."

"It is and I've brought it with me as promised," Booku said as he pointed to an old, battered attaché sitting at his feet.

I could readily relate to its badly abused condition. I'd spent many years working abroad with diplomatic title for the State Department with few rewards other than a bleeding ulcer and opportunity to participate in well-attended AA meetings. Hell, I didn't even get as much as a new briefcase when I retired.

"First, explain to me what's happening in Liberia. Your motives and intentions are clear—grab power and transfer the spoils of oil money to offshore banks for your early retirement nest egg. For what it's worth, we call those 401K accounts in the States. I understand that greed and power motivate you, that much is clear. I don't think it's a secret or inaccurate statement. Tell me I'm wrong."

"You're not. In fact, you could say you're right on the money, Mr. Dick. I want what others have wanted in the past. The developed nations don't understand Liberia or the continent in general. They talk about democracy and nation building as though they are things we Africans can relate to. We can't because we've only known poverty, government corruption, apathy, war, disease and incredible suffering. Do you think that the United States, Europe and the rest of the first-world countries would idly standby if the Darfur catastrophe were to be miraculously moved to let's say southern Europe or Central America?—how about Canada? I don't think so. In the West and elsewhere, we're still considered ignorant savages and sub-humans who also happen to be black—a perfect trifecta of prejudices and racial slurs. We're backward, illiterate bush niggers and nothing more to them."

Oh my God, Booku had just used the *N* word in my presence! My face immediately flushed from embarrassment since I'd never even say *niggardly* in mixed company for fear of offending someone. Although the word certainly applied to the paltry amount of money he was offering to sell-out my country. Regardless, I didn't want to come off as a redneck, white bread racist with no respect for the feelings of less fortunate colored people.

"But let me return to Liberia and your question," Booku continued. "Candidates for political office spew the meaningless platitudes about good governance and the like. But the people want food, safety and to be left alone to live their own lives. That's all and nothing more. Of course, when those same candidates take office they forget about the campaign promises and end-up lining their own pockets. That's the way it's been and that's the way it will always be. The people know that much. They accept it as a fact of life as much as the sun rising each morning."

"Do you know that one-third to one-half of the foreign assistance received by Liberia has been siphoned-off by its government officials? Who do you think these people are? They're cronies, friends and relatives of Ellen Sirleaf, that's who. They're members of her Unity Party, that's who. They're Liberians, that's who. They're Africans, that's who. Ellen's no different or better than her predecessors. The spoils of war and government office are one and the same."

Booku was getting pumped and agitated. I decided to let him vent rather than risk interrupting him. Not surprisingly, I chose discretion over valor once again.

"Even if what you say is true, the U.S. government loathes

supporting dictators. We have democratic principles to uphold and we vigorously promote them overseas. Our core values are totally incompatible with dictatorship," I smugly asserted.

Booku smugly laughed at my assertion.

"You have a great sense of humor but a poor memory and sense of geopolitics, Mr. Dick. Let me mention a few people to disabuse your naïve beliefs in the sanctity of your government's foreign affairs policies around the world."

"Here's a quick list: The Shah of Iran, Ferdinand Marcos, Manuel Noriega (before he double-crossed Uncle Sam), Fulgencio Batista, Rafael Trujillo, Augusto Pinochet, Pervez Musharraf, Juan Peron, and Saddam Hussein (before the wars). I'm sure I've forgotten a few. Do they ring any bells?"

They did, but it wasn't the Avon Lady standing on my mental doorstep. Notre Dame Cathedral sized ones rang out loud and clear but I wouldn't admit it to him. Regardless, he most likely had a good hunch that I wouldn't confess when my back was up.

"But none of those people are now in power," I countered. "Perhaps we've learned a lesson in leadership-by-example and the concept of universal human rights since then. Just maybe we've become a kinder, gentler nation under President Obama."

That brought another hearty laugh from my host. It seemed I was entertaining him. That certainly wasn't what I had in mind for our meeting although I enjoyed pleasing others with my subtle, sophisticated brand of humor. However, I had to be careful with casting witty pearls because I could be such a highbrowed swine and snob at times.

"My point of all of this is to illustrate that your country has supported dictatorships throughout its history. In a sense it still does; consider Egypt and Saudi Arabia. Egypt is the second largest recipient of American foreign aid, mostly military. When was the last fair and free election under Mubarak? The answer is there's never been one. Your government supports Mubarak because he's a powerful influence in the Arab world and pro-American given the generous assistance your nation provides to his country—a straightforward quid pro quo arrangement. The Saudis are your friends because of oil. In turn, they look to the States for the protection of their oil fields and refineries—another marriage of convenience. There's never been a national election in the country to my knowledge. How do those special relationships square with democracy building? The United States will deal with the Devil himself if it must."

"But what's that bottom line that you Americans keep talking about? Here it is: The United States does what it does out of pragmatic self-interest. The term is usually phrased as *in the national interest.* No matter, because they're both the same thing. Cozying up with military strongmen and other stripes of despots is sometimes necessary in America's national interest."

"Why are any of these things different from what I'm proposing? It's simply another quid pro quo arrangement in the interest of the United States. There's no guarantee that Ellen Sirlreaf or any of her successors will sell an ounce of oil to you. With me, you will have a written contract that I'll deliver what you want and desperately need to keep your economy strong."

Booku was running out of steam and now it was my turn to speak-up to vigorously counter his diatribe about United States foreign policy. I didn't do so and politely informed him I was tired and ready to go home. Although I'd have enough of his virulent, anti-American sentiment for one sitting, I couldn't manage to defend my country. I just didn't have the right stuff anymore.

My Uncle Sam would be terribly disappointed in me for what I was about to do. For God's sake, say it ain't so Avery! I wasn't about to be a good Joe.

"Booku, we have a deal! I'll back-off and you can go ahead with your bloody coup. You're right. I don't give a damn about Liberia or anyone but myself. My federal pension sucks and I can't even make ends meet with a supplemental social security check each month. I've spent many years working for my Uncle Sam and he's never appreciated the fact that I've put my life on the line for him on more than one occasion. It's now my turn to profit while I still can. Screw them all!"

Booku smiled as he handed me the attaché and headed the boat back to the dock. He said he would get in touch with me when the signed agreement was ready to be picked-up. I couldn't wait for his call or note because neither would arrive.

I didn't bother to suggest he add a little color to his face to tone down its countenance. A generous application of a nice crème blush might soften its stark white features. Truthfully, he might look a little more human if he had. Some anti-wrinkle lotion might also help with the scowl lines and jagged, battle scars. But, being a stubborn SOB, I refused to aid an enemy combatant either cosmetically or substantively. I had a reputation to uphold as a DS Special Agent in less-than-good standing.

Sadly, I was no longer a stand-up sort of guy. I'd fallen down on the job and let down the people that trusted me for so many years to do the right thing. I was at the nadir of my career and life but continued counting the money and counting the many ways I could spend it on myself. However, I was badly conflicted about what I'd done to myself, DS and my beloved country as I fantasized about my new Porsche Cayman and frequent trips to the fleshpots of Asia.

Sometimes those who protect and serve could be damn fine cosmetologists when staring death, treason, enormous car payments and painful STDs in the face.

Of course, my succumbing to greed and treason was just an act for Booku's benefit. But I still harbored strong cravings for the other things on my thoughtful wish list. Regardless, I wasn't about to let a fucking sociopathic war criminal escape justice because Liberia's future and America's honor were at stake. I wouldn't, couldn't disappoint my Uncle Sam. I'd never turn my back or coat on him for any reason. My bosom buddy and hero had never let me down before. Now it was my turn to defend him with all the resolve and vigor I could muster. I was a true red, white and blue patriot preparing for all-out war with a fearsome, formidable foe who was incapable of appreciating clever alliterations.

I couldn't recall how the *Battle Hymn of the Republic* went so I started humming *Onward Christian Soldier* as I walked to the car. Constitutionally, I knew it was wrong to combine church and state but I couldn't help myself. I also couldn't remember all of the hums so I had to wing it with a few by strumming some familiar riffs on my air guitar. Frank stared at me in amazement. He must have been awestruck by my performance because I was now walking ten feet off of 1600 Pennsylvania Avenue. My newly liberated wingtips lightly and spritely danced to the patriotic rhythms of the impromptu sole music. I was on cloud nine and not planning to come down anytime soon. But my hypoxia didn't last for long. Neither did my lithium carbonate for that matter.

Well, so much for all the blustering, bravado and funky, badass shuffling. I admitted that I was terrified of Booku and what lay ahead.

Sometimes those who protect and serve got an unnatural high from their own facetiousness and antidepressants; certainly not the pristine airs of the Rocky Mountains.

CHAPTER 16

DICKERING OVER OUR DILEMMA

As we drove home, I filled Frank in on my meeting with the monster man. I didn't reveal my fears and misgivings about the possibility of seeing him again. I showed him the attaché case and mentioned that I was now $50,000 richer. He was likely calculating his share. But he wouldn't get a dime because I planned to turn it over to the embassy. I would donate the money with the stipulation that it be used in good ways for the children of Monrovia. The State Department had never been especially charitable with me but I refused to hold a petty grudge. Nonetheless, I'd make sure to get a receipt for tax purposes. The proverb asserting that *charity begins at home* was a virtue I could easily live with.

I also told Frank about the nasty, little prank I pulled on Booku. As I got out of the boat, I clandestinely dropped a note in its bottom. Booku would discover it sooner or later and he'd go ballistic! Of course, that was the whole point of the exercise. Pulling his chain or pushing his buttons or making him go ballistic was all one in the same.

Borrowing a couple of sheets of Mary's lavender scented stationary, I'd written a note mimicking the tone and content of the one he'd sent me. Two could Tango or pimp as the case might be. My note was written in a clear hand so even Booku could read it without difficulty or squinting. I was very mindful of his medical condition. He was sightless but not blind, not a true visionary as far as I could see. Regardless, I wanted my message to rebut his outrageous proposals to sellout my country. Damn it, I wasn't an easy lay or cheap date these days!

We are at cross-purposes Mr. Beaucoup and needn't be. America doesn't need your bloody oil. Obviously, you don't share my short-term goal of hauling your butt to jail or putting a bullet through your brain. If you agree to surrender your sorry ass to me, I won't have to pay out 25 grand and we can both save my Uncle Sam some money. That's my generous offer. I should have offered far much less, you piece of shit. I'd like nothing better than to cut off your balls and shove them down your miserable throat until you choked to death. I delight in thinking of ways to kill you. Be aware, I have an overly active imagination and no compassion whatsoever for crazy fucks like you!

My government's support of Ellen Sirleaf is unwavering. We will take whatever measures are necessary to keep her in office. Democracy and freedom are values we cherish as Americans. Maybe we've grown up on TV shows where good always triumphed over evil. It doesn't matter because we are a people imbued with a strong sense of right and wrong and fair play. Simply put, we're Americans and damn proud of it!

Only one of us is a man of the world as you put it. Unlike you, I really do care for Liberia and its people. Humanity knows no boundaries. On the other hand, you embody the inhumanity in this world. You're an insane sadist who must die. If you need any help, I'm here for you!

FUCK YOU ASSHOLE!!!

In God we trust. May He or She continue to bless America, the home of the free and the brave!

Very truly yours,
Avery M. Dick III, DS Special Agent (Ret.)

Of course, the State Department didn't tolerate the use of coarse language in its fastidious, diplomatic discourses. However, its less than diplomatic Diplomatic Security Service sometimes encouraged it—*get on the fucking ground sleazebag, you're under arrest!*

Sometimes those who protect and serve grudgingly acknowledged that talk was cheap, actions spoke louder than words and trite expressions were a dime a dozen.

The UNMIL vehicle was neatly boxed-in at a busy downtown intersection. The driver didn't have a chance to execute any defensive maneuvers to escape the trap, even if he knew how to. It was a quick, clean *grab and run* operation at gunpoint. The Bangladeshi UN driver was pulled from the vehicle and shot three times in the chest at very close range. He died where he fell. Two attackers jumped into the car and sped away. Mary Tambo was sitting by herself in the backseat.

Mary had returned to work two days earlier and was on a light schedule until she fully regained her strength. She was heading to a routine meeting at one of the many United Nations buildings in the city on the day she was hijacked. Witnesses reported the woman in the back of the car was waving her arms and gesturing with her middle finger. I was positive Mary was giving her captors an earful of righteous indignation. In her case, the bird was the word.

The UNMIL vehicle was later found abandoned and empty a few miles past the ELWA Junction on the road to the airport. The local scavengers were already picking over its carcass. It seemed that Booku had no sense of humor and was exacting his revenge by kidnapping Mary. But there was no doubt that I was his ultimate prize. I guessed the honeymoon was over without as much as a perfunctory consummation. It looked like I still had to wait for the climax—Booku's painful death. Love wasn't always forever or necessarily a splendid thing in Africa.

Sometimes those who protect and serve didn't care whether they had rough sex *in flagrante delicto* or Liberia.

According to Frank, Booku was dead in the water. Unfortunately, he wasn't in any literal sense but only figuratively speaking. The literal meaning would soon come if I had my way. Frank's sources reported that our efforts had completely undercut the support for his nefarious venture into the most uncivil affairs of the country. Uncle Fred's taboo had tipped the scale in our favor. Booku was out of business, well almost. He had Mary and I didn't have him. The United Nations and Liberian National Police would be useless in locating Mary and securing her release. Moreover, their bungling efforts might get her killed in any hostage rescue operation. But Ellen Sirleaf and her government were now home free. Mary wasn't as fortunate but I planned for her homecoming just the same. I was still deciding on the party favors.

Frank lent me an old, but serviceable, snub-nosed Smith & Wesson model 60 revolver and some .38 caliber rounds for it. He said it was untraceable. That meant he'd swiped it from the SSS armory and destroyed any and all inventory records. It wasn't an accurate weapon at a distance of more than 10 feet. Also, it only held five bullets compared to 18 in the magazine of my Glock but it would have to do. I couldn't ask for another gun from Phil because there would be too many uncomfortable questions. I'd have to bite that old bullet again. My left canine was starting to ache in anticipation.

While we waited for Booku to contact me, I had Frank ask the Oma to use her influence with the Liberian cops and tell them to back-off any investigation of Mary's kidnapping. Information of her whereabouts would be appreciated but nothing else. If pressed, she could explain that the United Nations police were the lead agency given the circumstances. The assertion was logical and plausible up to a point. However, the Liberian police and security apparatus had not completely rolled over and played dead in subservient deference to their UN masters. They often were able to avoid its big thumb they labored under and go about their business without their Big Brother's knowledge and consent. Maybe they'd pick up something useful on our behalf and not share it with their witless, clueless mentors. That would work to our advantage and perhaps keep Mary alive.

Regardless, baby blue berets were no longer fashionable among the people in Liberia. The fad had gradually faded within a couple of years of introduction because they had worn thin. They were no longer considered de rigueur for the rigors and realities facing ordinary citizens. It was time for them to be packed up and shipped elsewhere. Hopefully, others might find them to be a more effective head cover when the sky was falling.

There were two things that I was confident of at this point: Mary was still alive and that Booku would contact me fairly soon. Of those, I could be absolutely certain. He wouldn't kill her just yet because she was the bright lure to hook and reel me into his net. But I didn't intend to be an easy catch. By the way, there was no such thing as a *catch and release* policy in this biz.

Sometimes those who protect and serve couldn't explain the goodwill generated by the world's salvation army.

CHAPTER 17

OUR GRIM REAPER COMETH

Booku's call came at about 6 AM. I was deep in sleep figuring out all of the vicious ways I could kill the bastard. *How do I hate thee? Let me count the ways motherfucker,* flashed through my brain. I mentally added the crime of inconsiderate, rude behavior to his long list of crimes against humanity.

"That wasn't very nice of you," Booku spoke. "Just like your country, you have no honor or balls. In good faith, I offered America a deal that would have ensured its independence from Middle East oil. But you insultingly threw the offer back in my face. You double-crossed me. That was a mistake on your part, Mr. Dick. You can play the hero but it doesn't change the fact that your country has just lost a great opportunity for a cheap, dependable source of energy for at least a decade. Your economy's already in a deep slump and your arrogant and foolish decision will further exacerbate the problem. Congratulations, you're a real dick, my friend!"

"You'll be glad to learn I'm leaving Liberia for good. Your efforts to thwart my plans worked, again congratulations and kudos. I no longer have any support for my cause thanks to you. But we both still have some unfinished business to take care of. Don't we? That business is Mary Tambo and the $50,000 you stole from me the other night. By the way, that was a good performance that you put on for my benefit. It fooled me and I'm not easily fooled. I can assure you that I won't make a similar mistake again. What's the saying, once burned, twice shy? I'm not the slightest bit shy and now it's your turn to get burned, you miserable prick teaser."

"Here's my new deal and it's not negotiable. If you want to save Ms. Tambo, you'll meet me tonight at 11 PM sharp at the Monrovia Port on Bushrod Island. Come directly to pier 2. I'll be aboard the *Kobayashi Maru* that sails at midnight. Don't bother informing the authorities because you won't be able to locate Mary without my help. I can be so recalcitrant at times, even under robust torture. That's one of the many advantages of insanity. I enjoy pain, either giving or getting! Sadomasochism runs through my veins and oozes from my pores. Not to brag, but I devised some of the techniques the police now routinely use to tease the truth. At least I have that much of a legacy to be proud of."

"Oh, I also want a hundred grand for Mary. That's in addition to my money. Why didn't you mention that she's one sizzling hot bitch? Have you had a taste yet? I'll bet she's sweet! Don't worry, I promise not to kill or seriously injure her. But I have every right to do so considering what she did to me with her Uncle Fred's help. Are you surprised by my generosity? You shouldn't be because where I'm going she'll fetch top dollar in the white slave trade. She'll be a haggard, diseased whore within a year," Booku lasciviously laughed.

I'd stayed silent during Booku's crazy talk but couldn't hold my tongue any longer after he mentioned what might happen to Mary. Yet I wondered if all of Mary's visas and shots were up-to-date and in good order. Immigration officers could be real sticklers for petty detail!

"Booku, if you touch a hair of Mary, either above or below the waist, you'll have to answer to me!" I was absolutely furious, seething with anger. Booku had finally gotten to me with that threat. I couldn't abide the thought of someone other than myself defiling her perfectly toned body. I had first dibs, damn it!

Booku laughed at my silly, pretentious statement. Actually, I found he could be fairly affable and outgoing at times.

Be there or be square were his last words before hanging up the phone. The guy definitely had a weird thing for banal colloquialisms and bloody coups. Maybe he should've mounted a war of words instead.

Sometimes those who protect and serve got red in the face and green with envy, but never yellow, at the same time.

Frank and I reviewed our options. The task didn't take long because there were few or less. We weren't about to notify the authorities and jeopardize our chance to save Mary from a life of shame and forced debauchery along with making a ton of money thorough gentlemen with generous tips. We both knew Mary wouldn't stand for it and I wouldn't take it lying down. It looked like we were betwixt and between again. However, neither of us budged or sacrificed our firmly held positions; the maneuvering was much too awkward for both of us. It was a classic Mexican standoff held on foreign soil.

Frank quickly learned that the *Kobayashi Maru* was a Liberian registered ship and it indeed was in port and scheduled to sail tonight. It was a tramp steamer and its notional ports of call included Accra, Lome, Lagos, Libreville and points south. It was destined to sail around the Cape of Good Hope and then head-up the coast of East Africa. I wondered if Booku chose the ship out of a strong sense of irony given Mary's prospects of working on her back. Regardless, I prayed that her owner and/or pimp would treat her with the respect she deserved.

But concerning Booku, he wasn't clever or prescient enough to see the small irony in the ship's class. If he had been, he'd have worked-out an exit strategy that didn't involve risk to his own safety. Had he converted to Islam, he could have sought sanctuary in Saudi Arabia like the infamous Ugandan dictator, Idi Amin Dada—birds or ghouls of a feather?

It wasn't the least bit surprising that the *Kobayashi Maru* was registered in Liberia. You could've flipped a coin and had a slightly better than 25% chance of being right. That was because more than 50% of all *flag of convenience* ships in the world were registered in Liberia. Panama was a close second but still no cigar. Liberia now had more registered ships than the United States.

The term had been around since the 50s to identify those vessels whose owners' nationalities differed from the countries of registration. It was done to reduce an owner's operating cost by avoiding pesky government regulations governing such things as taxes, safety and crew wages. The owner of the *Kobayashi Maru* was no different. Maybe the international admiralty laws also protected those who tried to overthrow democratically elected governments too. Anything was possible under the right circumstances, right? Sadly, only endless, unpredictable possibilities, not opportunities, abounded for the Liberian people.

Sometimes those who protect and serve weren't always in shipshape condition and able to shiver their own timbers while lumbering for answers to life's knotty problems.

Frank drove me to the port ahead of our appointed hour. We parked a good distance away and walked the rest of the way on foot while watching our steps. We'd need to retrace them later if we lived. Fortunately, there were no mishaps or missteps along the way to the port. We had no difficulty getting inside the fenced facility with Frank's credentials and the M-4 rifle slung over his right shoulder. The duffle bag he carried simply added to his mystique. We were welcomed like long-lost brothers by the security guards who must have been bored to tears and looked forward to any small respite from the tedium. The smallest things out of the ordinary provided for good street theatre for Liberians. They had too much time on their hands and nowhere to spend it productively.

No one paid attention to my darkened visage under the skullcap I'd worn for the occasion. I had liberally applied charcoal to my face and hands and I now looked like a bona fide African-American with a noticeable complexion disorder. But my blue eyes might pose a small problem. Sooner or later, I'd have to face the consequences of my handiwork. But for now, it was the best disguise I could come up with on short notice. *Comeuppance* wasn't one of my favorite words unless it applied to others. However, it might just fool an out-of-sight monster bent on my destruction.

I was carrying the same briefcase Booku had given me earlier during our negotiations; sorry, I meant to say conversations. Conversations were okay under U.S. policy when dealing with terrorists and kidnappers; negotiations weren't. Again, it was the *distinction without a difference* phenomenon that worked so well in Washington. I'd have to introduce the federal bureaucrats to the concept of African-style palavering. Jeez, that would really stir the pot and make things interesting!

Jane, please remind me of my 3 o'clock appointment. I have some serious palavering to do with my bosses on the 7th floor. I'm the designated palaverer for the meeting so I can't be late. Hold all my calls unless they're about the palaver. I don't have time for meaningless small talk today! I don't want to talk to my ex-wife either. Also, please fix me another cup of coffee. This time don't forget to bring a napkin sweetie.

Sensitivity, gender relations and latent anger management training was never part of the DS curriculum for those up-and-coming Dicks who protect and serve.

I started laughing when I first saw the *Kobayashi Maru.* That helped relieve my tension a bit. It was a rust encrusted hulk of metal that obviously had seen much better days. Its paint had badly peeled in many places and looked like a snake sloughing-off its old skin. Maybe its last port of call on this trip would be the scrap yard in Mombasa. In any case, Booku was not going out in style.

My cell phone rang and I answered knowing that Booku had my number. I prayed that it wasn't up just yet because I still had to rescue Mary and save America's reputation.

"Mr. Dick, you're five minutes late," Booku chided. Time is money and I don't see all of mine this time. I see my briefcase but nothing more. Where's the additional hundred grand I instructed you to bring for Mary's life? By the way, did you forget to shave and wash your face? You look sickly. If you have something contagious, tell me right now."

Well, so much for my not-so-clever disguise. My face reddened at my unmasking but no one would notice my embarrassment. That was due to good tradecraft by covering my face with the charcoal. The dark arts had come through again and had served a useful purpose after all. I quickly regained my composure and wiped off my loss of face. I also pulled up my pants a notch to show everyone who was in charge of this situation. I hated not being in control under conditions that I couldn't control in the slightest. It was one of my little quirks that surfaced when my life was in serious danger of being snuffed-out.

However, I ignored Booku's chivvying and untimely remark. He was probably using a pair of high-powered binoculars to scan the pier. But he seemed to be in a big hurry. The ship's captain was likely pressuring him to quickly conclude our little *tete-a-tete* and toe-to-toe so he could depart on schedule. Peer pressure could be so intimidating at times, especially for sea captains carrying perishable cargoes and sailing on-the-clock around the clock.

"Take a look twenty yards behind me and to the right. You'll see a large duffle bag at the feet of my colleague." Frank had earlier broken down his M-4 and placed it in the bag.

"No, I'm not sick, only suffering from a mild case of stupidity, what you Liberians call *anal-cranial inversion,* but thanks anyway for asking. That was very considerate under the circumstances. Since you inquired about my health, I also want you to know that I don't suffer from hypochondria except when I'm meeting a sick, fucking sociopath who wants me dead. Then every little concern is magnified tenfold for purposes of self-preservation."

Booku must have accepted my unhealthy explanation for coming to the party in blackface but very much out of costume. Regardless, sound diagnostic gibberish and wisdom couldn't be challenged, especially in medically underserved Liberia.

"Okay, come aboard, but only you Mr. Dick. Captain Yamaguchi has kindly lowered the gangway so you can board. I'll be amidships in his stateroom on the second deck awaiting your arrival. Don't try anything stupid or Mary Tambo will die."

It seemed it was now *do or die* time. Fortunately, I was a dyed-in-the-wool doer from the get-go. Doing things was never a problem for me during my career. However, doing them safely and correctly was more problematic.

Frank escorted me to the stairway. I didn't bother to take the duffle bag and Booku would be unable to see that I'd left it behind. I climbed the plank and was now on the ship's top deck. The gangway immediately pulled back from the dock and folded onto the ship. I looked around and found an open hatchway and entered. The place was deserted. It was a ghost ship, a fitting place for a ghoul to hide. I suspected the captain and crew were in the ship's hold and far away from any action that might occur. If things went to shit, they could claim they were conducting a pre-departure briefing and hadn't heard or seen a thing. That little Kabuki dance would at least keep the authorities guessing what might have happened.

I walked down a passageway until I found a set of stairs. Booku was one level below and in the center of the ship. I was getting close to my destiny. I also was starting to get seasick or maybe experiencing the onset of a panic attack. I couldn't be sure but I wasn't feeling so well at the moment. However, I was about to feel much worse!

As I reached the second deck, someone grabbed me from behind and put a strong chokehold on me. I was kept in check by my attacker's forearm around my neck. We struggled and slammed each other into the narrow passageway walls. We repeatedly banged each others' bodies trying to get an upper hand on the other. He was winning the match because I couldn't loosen his death grip. I often got choked-up at close, intimate times like these.

I finally bent both of us forward and grabbed the back of his calves. I pulled hard and we both fell backwards to the floor. That was enough to loosen his hold. I quickly reversed positions and sat on his chest with all of my 240 pounds of sinewy muscle. I removed my Smith 60 from my waist and placed its nose in the center of his forehead and pulled the trigger but nothing happened. I tried a second and third time with the same result. I'd hoped to put a bullet right through the fucker's pineal gland because I couldn't easily reach his prostate. The third eye effect might give him some enlightenment before he died. I threw the revolver down the passageway in disgust.

The ammunition was bad given the fact it had been left for so many years to corrode in the high humidity of an armory without air conditioning. I was thoroughly familiar with duds having spent so many years working for the State Department. Most I met were old, corrosive assholes that couldn't shoot straight, even from the hip.

I continued to sit on my attacker's chest and lit up a Marlboro to ponder the meaning of life. His squirming didn't help to dislodge him or interrupt my thoughts. His face turned red and his eyes bulged from their sockets. I smoked another cigarette because my ponderings hadn't revealed any wisdom. I was just as confused about the cosmos and women as before. However, my charge's movements had now greatly lessened and his face was turning blue. Apparently, he couldn't catch a breath or break to save his life.

I sat some more but didn't smoke because I knew it could be hazardous to my health. However, smoking was very low on my list of things to worry about at the moment. My attacker had stopped all movement a couple of minutes earlier. He wasn't breathing and his bulging eyes were open and fixed. I was happy that the last thing they saw was the shit-eating grin on my face. Burking was an extremely unpleasant way to die but he deserved it. Regardless, Moses Kekula had just expired. He no longer had any more aspirations in this life.

Frank would be furious that I'd killed Moses because he was looking forward to doing it himself. I'd have to figure out a way to pay him back in kind.

Those sedentary, fat-assed Dicks who sometimes protect and serve occasionally enjoyed throwing their weight around.

Booku must have thought I'd gotten lost. But I made my way to the captain's stateroom a minute later. We were both operating on Liberian time so my delay wouldn't seem too unusual. However, in the meantime, I believed the ship's captain was still using Greenwich. He was going to sail come Hell or high water. I didn't have much time left.

The door was open and I walked-in unannounced. It wasn't proper decorum but I no longer cared for upholding petty protocols. Booku wasn't the least bit surprised, either at my arrival or egregious social gaffe. He sat in a far chair facing the door and was dressed in black from his beret to his leather loafers. Booku was a colorful dresser if you were into basic black. Now, this was the feared Booku I'd heard so much about rather than the Mickey Mouse caricature I'd met on the boat. Other than some errant flecks of lint on his clothes, he was dressed to kill or ready for a funeral. I'd take my own pick.

"What took you so long and where's the duffle bag?" He was

clenching both his teeth and the upside-down cross hanging from his neck. He didn't appear to be in good humor given his demeanor and non-white uniform. But I didn't give a rat's ass.

"You're welcoming party slowed me up a bit and the duffle bag is safely sitting on the top deck. It was too heavy to carry along with the attaché case. You should have asked for less money and maybe you'd have it now."

I goofed with him by making one arm appear longer than the other. He didn't appreciate my feeble attempt to disarm him and break the ice.

"What are you talking about with the 'welcoming party' crap?"

"Moses Kekula stopped to chat me up in the passageway. He wanted to say hello and wring my neck like a chicken. That's what I'm talking about. Booku, you can't be trusted if your or my life depended on it. We were to meet and exchange money for Mary and nothing more. It was to be a straightforward business deal; quid pro quo, as you like to say. Well, I've brought the money but I don't see Mary Tambo. We're not *even-Steven* or *eye-to-eye* or however you describe *fucking me over* in this one-sided arrangement."

I could be such a vicious bitch when I got my back up! However, spewing truly vile language wasn't in my heart or vocabulary. I was invariably speechless and mute when it came to such nasty things.

"Moses wasn't supposed to harm you. I'd made that point perfectly clear to him earlier. I told him that any harm to you would come from my hands. He acted in bad faith and against my explicit orders. Good help is hard to find in Liberia these days," he chuckled. "Mary's quite safe. She's busy preparing for a sea cruise at the moment so you'll have to excuse her rude absence. Don't worry. The salt air will do her good."

Booku was yanking my chain, busting my chops or pulling my pud. Regardless, they all were painful, frustrating experiences. The meeting was going nowhere less than fast. I didn't have a gun to threaten Booku's life and force him to tell me where Mary was. It turned out that I needed one.

While checking the shine on my shoes, Booku pulled a cutlass from the sofa he was sitting next to and came towards me. That was enough for me to beat a hasty exit out the door and down the passageway. I leapt over Moses' body as I retreated to other, safer parts of the ship. Despite my paunch and overweight condition, I was still able to outrun Booku. My adrenaline must have been in better chemical shape than his. That was because I'd worked-out with it so often during my long, frightful career as a DS special agent.

I had ditched Booku, at least for the time being. I'd moved to the stern of the ship and waited there to catch my breath. I still hadn't spotted anyone else on the ship and that reinforced my suspicion that the captain and crew had battened-down the hatches and were waiting out the storm above them.

With my elbow, I smashed the glass cover to the wall-mounted cabinet holding a flare gun. The gun was heavy and I knew it held only one flare. It was at least something to defend myself with. I'd never fired one before despite my many emergencies, personal and otherwise. I couldn't tap out an SOS signal either so I was screwed blue without as much as a tattoo to show for it. While hiding, I mused about guns and their descending number of rounds—18, 5 and now 1. I'd probably save the last one for me. It would still be preferable to what Booku had in mind for my demise. *One* was the loneliest number as they said. For the first time, I understood what *they* meant.

My reverie was interrupted by footsteps and the slashing sound of Booku's machete as he walked past my hidey-hole. I was in a janitorial closet and the pungent fumes from the solvents were making me lightheaded and dizzy, perhaps more than usual. After he passed a distance, I made a dash for the stairs. He caught my movement and chased me to the top deck. He was panting heavily like the wild animal he was.

I ran to the far rear of the ship and had nowhere else to go. Booku caught up with me and we circled each other like wrestlers in a grudge match. I only hoped it wouldn't turn out to be a tag team event. I had the flare gun at the ready as he sliced the air just in front of me. The blade of the machete just missed my right arm.

No words were exchanged between us; it was too late for talk. As he rounded me again, I steadied the gun with both hands and fired. The incendiary round hit Booku squarely in the chest, a bull's-eye. Despite my shaking, I couldn't have missed from 10 feet. His entire chest lit up like a thousand candles in the darkness. The entry wound burning through his body would be the size of a half dollar. More importantly, it would be fatal. I didn't get a chance to measure its diameter because his body immediately did a half gainer over the deck's railing. I heard it hit the water with a splash.

I then looked down and saw part of the flare still burning on top of the water. Booku's corpse had quickly sunk to the bottom of the deep. "Good riddance to bad rubbish," I exultantly and vehemently yelled to the water. Now Davey Jones would have a new playmate. Booku's body would surface in a few days as putrefaction caused its gasses to expand. For what it was worth, he didn't have an ounce of spiritual buoyancy in him. At some point, a fisherman or kid on a beach would discover it and notify the authorities. No matter, a human monster had been slain on an errant night in darkest Liberia.

Sometimes those who protect and serve had a flare for the dramatic but no nautical sense whatsoever.

Booku's ship had finally sailed, but Mary's vessel still worried me. I carefully searched the upper decks of the *Kobayashi Maru* for the next 20 minutes without finding her or anybody else. I called her name a few times to no avail as I walked about. I was beginning to wonder if she were already dead. Booku wasn't a man of his word, but then again neither was I. Funny we had at least one trait in common.

I made my way to the lower bowels of the ship and it didn't

take long to locate the captain and crew. As I walked the fourth deck, I heard them laughing and talking in one of the cargo bays. I could also hear a radio or CD deck playing Japanese music. As I entered, two crewmen ungraciously threw me to the floor. *Oh God,* I thought, *not again please.* I'd had enough fighting and violence for one night. I was exhausted and simply wanted to go home to my bed. I didn't struggle with them because I was too damned tired. I also didn't know jujutsu, aikido, haiku or any of the Japanese martial arts so once again I was at a major disadvantage. Other than the cordial greeting *Hi,* I couldn't speak a word of their language.

As I lamented my poor language skills, I heard a short burst of gunfire. The music abruptly stopped and the room went silent. I looked up and saw Frank holding his M-4 in the combat firing stance. He'd just murdered the shortwave radio sitting innocently on a crate in the corner. I suspected that Frank would eventually have to face the music for what he'd rashly done in a fit of anger. Fortunately for him, crimes of passion were often forgiven in Liberia. I wasn't so sure about Japan though.

About the same time, a young sailor made the foolish mistake of rushing Frank with a small pocket knife. Frank slapped him across the face with the butt of his weapon. The young fellow fell backwards and screamed in pain. He should've known that it wasn't called an assault rifle for nothing. The rest of the crew, including the captain, rose to their feet and politely bowed to Frank. Apparently, he had gotten their undivided attention and undying respect. I was amazed by his facility in Japanese!

I unsteadily stood and asked the captain where Mary was being held. He bowed to me and pointed to a closed hatch at the far end of the bay. I went to the door while Frank covered my back. I opened it and found Mary lying on an old mattress in her own urine and feces. I removed her blindfold and gag and held her close despite the odor. My frisky, right hand accidently brushed-up against her pert breasts, smooth thighs and tight buttocks. She wasn't carrying a concealed weapon. I reluctantly acknowledged later that a pat-down wasn't necessary under the circumstances. However, sometimes old, DS training habits came in handy.

I told her she was okay and that everything would be fine. Booku was dead and our jobs in Liberia were over. We both could now go home with our heads held high. She was disoriented and the lights from the outer room caused her eyes to squint. Obviously, she'd been cooped-up too long with the crew. Mary seemed to be okay physically but her emotional state might be a different story. We'd have to wait and see. Regardless, she was now safe and in good hands.

Tora! Tora! Tora! Those words boomed inside my head! Jeez, I couldn't think straight when my dander was up or I'd been nipping too much. We thanked our hosts for their hospitality by rudely telling them we thought the Koreans and Chinese were kicking the shit out of Japanese consumer products. They were wounded by the vile accusation and would never forgive us for the nationalistic slight and loss of face. I didn't care since I didn't plan to vacation in Hawaii anytime soon. However, it was time to disembark and get the hell off the ship. Frank now took the gangway instead of having to shinny the ship's mooring rope as he'd done earlier.

We all looked forward to a good nights' sleep knowing that a hideous creature had been killed and would no longer haunt our dreams or those of the Liberian people.

Sometimes those who protect and serve found night terrors could also be cured by a clear conscience, a few glasses of wine and a couple of mega-dose tranquilizers.

CHAPTER 18

RESTING ON OUR LAZY LAURELS

Oh Avery, you're my hero! Mary exclaimed. I thought I was a goner until you arrived to save my worthless, but beautifully honed butt. God, where are all the other strong, masculine men of this world? Most are merely wannabes compared to you. How can I repay you? Words don't seem to be adequate at a time like this. How about some hot, kinky sex instead? What turns you on baby? Tell me your innermost desires and positions. I'll pleasure you in ways that you've only dreamed about.

By the way, have you had your annual prostate exam? No? Shame on you Avery Dick for ignoring your health at your age! Don't worry. Your overly plump tushie is now in the good hands of Nurse Nancy. Okay, where was I? Oh yeah, maybe I can get one of my girlfriends to play too. Your wish is my command and I really dig being commanded by a stud-hunk like you. How about we............

"Avery, you're a fucking dick!"

My vivid daydream about Mary had just been coitus-interrupted by Phil's shrill voice. My daydreams were getting longer and more detailed in my old age. Fortunately, I didn't suffer from diurnal emissions yet. Those would've been seminally embarrassing and only jack-up my dry cleaning bill. Besides, I'd already had my fill of seamen for a lifetime.

"Why didn't you cut us in to what you were doing here? Damn it, this is our backyard and you've embarrassed the shit out of us. Same for you Frank, you should've known better!"

Mary, Frank, the American ambassador, Phil Jensen, Jackson Smyth, the embassy security attaché, and I were sitting in the VIP waiting room outside the president's office. I didn't respond to Phil's question because it would only further enrage him. Jeez, wait until he heard about my missing Glock! He fully realized that I'd pulled the wool-over-his-eyes and he was smarting from its itching sensation. Phil now knew there would be no kudos for the great job he claimed he'd done in Liberia. He appeared to be one sad pup that had been kicked once too often while it was lying down. That description pretty well summed up my DS career as well.

Of course, the ambassador, Ms. Primrose Lane didn't come to my defense. She kept silent and to herself. That was understandable because she was a political appointee and not a career ambassador. Old school Foreign Service officers generally would confess their complicity and foreknowledge under such circumstances. They would readily do so to share the fame and glory of a success; otherwise they'd claim they weren't in the loop. In fact, they couldn't even see the loop. What's a loop, they'd politely but disingenuously ask? It seemed that none had ever visited Chicago, especially in the winter when it was easy to get snowed.

However, Primrose had earned her striped pants in a different manner. She'd been active in the Republican Party and a regular, although meagerly, contributor to its causes over the years. That meant she'd bought her office through campaign contributions and party favors. Lucky for her, the bidding for the Liberian posting had also been meager. Regardless, I thought she got shortchanged in the deal. That didn't speak well for her conversational or negotiating skills.

Our private audience with President Sirleaf would be short but very sweet. We were slotted for only five minutes of her busy time. However, that would be enough for Phil and Jackson to swallow their pride and repeatedly stick their fingers down their throats when no one was looking.

Sometimes those who protect and serve got a chance to toot their own horn and strut-their-stuff in front of jealous colleagues who wanted nothing but the same recognition.

We were ushered single file into her private office and, following the pro forma introductions and greetings, were told to sit. I hoped we didn't have to roll over, beg and play dead too! That would be too much ceremony for one sitting.

"You have done a great service for our country and each of you is to be commended and congratulated!" Ellen Sirleaf spoke in a strong voice.

She was dressed in a colorful caftan and headscarf and had a physical presence that dominated the room.

"You have rid our nation of a terrible threat that could have caused our democratic institutions and personal freedoms to be lost once again. The Liberian people have suffered too much already. But through your accomplishments, we have the chance to rebuild our country into a role model for all of Africa. Those that cherish liberty and freedom may one day look to Liberia as an example to emulate."

"Please stand." Everyone did as ordered.

"Mary Tambo, Frank Yeaten and Avery Dick, please come forward." We all did as told. While doing so, three of the president's aides moved in front of us and opened small leather-bound cases.

"As President of the Republic of Liberia, I hereby confer the Order of the African Star on each of you for your outstanding service. It is the nation's second highest honor to be bestowed on anyone. Please accept my personal congratulations and thanks as well. We won't forget what you've done to help us."

I wondered what the highest honor could be and what one might have to do to earn it. If it had anything to do with it being only awarded posthumously, I wasn't in the least interested.

The president then shook our hands indicating the ceremony was over. The aides collected our medals and mentioned they'd be kept in the building's vault for safekeeping. We could come by anytime to take a peek at them as long as we had a personal approval from the president.

I then realized that Liberia had adopted another Americanism—plausible denial. Not surprisingly, no photographs of the ceremony or its participants were taken by the MFA publicity office. They must have been busy with a more important photo-op. A press release was out of the question under the circumstances.

Phil shot me a dirty scowl as I headed to the lift. Not to be outdone, I stuck out my tongue and wiggled it back and forth to show him I wasn't the least bit intimidated. As close buds, we fingered each other before going our own ways.

Sometimes those who protect and serve much preferred the pomp and circumstance to the pimp and pout.

Mary, Frank and I celebrated by having dinner at the Palm Restaurant. Phil and Jackson weren't invited since they were busy licking their psychic wounds. Perceived snubs and slights could be so hurtful.

We ordered champagne but I would have preferred Zinfandel. But I was polite and didn't say anything rude or obnoxious. After all, it was a joyful occasion to share stories and reflect on what we had accomplished. It was also good therapy and a way to decompress. Mary was still a bit shaky after her ordeal and needed time to deal with her emotional problems. I kindly decided not to share my daydream so as not to excite or frighten her as the case might be. I could play the role of a gentleman when need be, but not for very long. My multiple personalities were too rambunctious to keep in check indefinitely. They continually argued as to which one would emerge next. Jeez, they needed to take a number and get a life! The bickering got so intense that I eventually paid them no mind. In the end, it was all about self discipline.

We laughed and joked the entire evening but some of the back-and-forth bantering seemed forced and hollow. I suspected Frank and I would have our own emotional issues to deal with after the high wore off. Unlike Booku, we were both human. We said our goodnights and went our separate ways. Despite exchanging contact numbers and addresses, we likely wouldn't speak or see each other again. Reminiscences, as well as snubs and slights, could be so hurtful.

I still had some loose ends to tie-up before leaving Liberia. In Amos Brown's case, *untying* would be more accurate. He hadn't spilled his guts or the beans but neither mattered. He was no longer necessary and now expendable property.

I ordered Amos' release knowing full well what was in store for him. But I didn't have any control or choice in the matter. His guards had to cover all of their bases, tracks and asses. I didn't feel particularly good about what I'd done and didn't sleep well. Even the almonds seemed to scold me with their incessant droppings.

Sometimes those who protect and serve deserved to be lauded, feted and damned to Hell on the same day.

CHAPTER 19

BOTHERSOME BOOMERANGS

My *To Do* list was getting shorter by the day. I'd dropped off Booku's 50 grand with the embassy cashier and she did give me a receipt. As paymaster for the caper, I settled-up with the surviving NBI agents and Amos Brown's jailers. I also gave a generous stipend to the widow of the NBI agent who was killed at the stadium and even to Amos Brown's wife. Maybe I'd sleep a little better by doing so. My conscience was still bothering me and I needed to give it a rest. Neither Moses Kekula's estate nor his widow would receive a dime. My generosity could only be pushed so far. My guilt even less so in Moses' case.

I'd decided to move to the Mamba Point Hotel tomorrow for a mental break and a little TLC. It had four stars and I planned to be one of them for a couple of days while I sorted out my ticketing and travel arrangements. I was still trying to figure out how to get around the rule that I had to fly home economy rather than business class. I'd come up with something plausible so later I could deny any intentional defalcation. I was simply following the standard government practices of obfuscation and disingenuousness. I was a very compliant, conscientious employee when it came to such things.

Sometimes those who protect and serve pushed an organization's envelope from time-to-time but never remained stationary for long.

The newspapers had stopped raping and pillaging Booku's character and reputation. The editors had been compensated too. However, speculation still continued about his intentions and whereabouts. I smiled when I read the fanciful theories and explanations by the press. His body hadn't surfaced yet but soon would. Mother Nature would do her job in her good time and place. Some things in life are immutable and others didn't change either. The ocean currents and tides were one example of that certainty. Booku would finally be washed-up and beached for good.

I took a last swim in the compound's large pool before packing my bags and heading to the Mamba Point Hotel. The warm water soothed my aching muscles and helped me unwind and relax. The nagging pains in my butt and neck were beginning to recede. The bar at the hotel would help the process along. The full body massage later would result in a blissful, happy ending.

Sea Suites was deserted, not surprising since it was a regular work day for most folks. Phil and the advisors were toiling away at whatever they did to justify their outrageous salaries. Others working for the UN were sitting at their desks thinking up things to do to and ways to spend money on Liberia and themselves. However, I was totally alone for the first time in weeks and I reveled in the experience.

Sometimes those who protect and serve yearned for nothing more than privacy and the chance to properly fold their tent before going home.

I opened the door to my apartment and immediately noticed

how cold it was. My swim had cooled me off and the air conditioner was running at full blast. Maybe I sensed something more chilling in the air. I had and I froze in fear. Jesus Christ! Merci Beaucoup was standing in my living room dressed in a security guard's uniform. My jaw, balls and confidence all dropped at the same time. My knees also weakened and I had to put my back to the door to support me.

I'd just seen a ghastly ghost! It couldn't really be Booku because I saw him die. Did he have a twin or doppelganger? I was in shock and awe despite being in Liberia. Maybe I'd sprinkled too much oregano on my spaghetti marinara last night. In any event, I was now looking in the face of death; it was contorted, pale white and sneering.

"You're dead. I saw you die!" I screamed at the top of my lungs. The bottoms of my lungs had been impaired by years of heavy smoking so they couldn't contribute much in the way of force and volume. I probably should have said *I gasped* instead.

Booku laughed at my outburst and girlish sounding declarations. His laugh actually sounded more mechanical than maniacal. Maybe the guy had been resurrected as a robot or android instead of a human monster.

With his free hand, he unbuttoned his shirt and opened it for me to see. He was holding a pistol in his other hand. Underneath his shirt was a black vest and I could make out a pronounced white blob in the center where the flare's phosphorous round struck. I hadn't missed after all, small comfort given my present situation.

"As we both know, Kevlar is truly a miracle product, Mr. Dick. The body armor not only stops bullets but is a highly effective heat shield and flame retardant used in firefighters clothing. By the way, the flare knocked the wind out of me and I almost drowned."

I sincerely commiserated with his plight. Someone later explained what *commiserated* meant. I still wasn't sure about *plight* though. More of the confusing Liberian-English crap no doubt.

"But so much for the pleasantries, let's move on. You're about to die a painful, horrible death. It's the least I can do to repay you for your many kindnesses. Let me describe it to you in colorful, blood red detail. I'm sure you'll find it educational and amusing."

Booku removed his sunglasses and I knew then he wasn't joking. There were no diamond chips lining his orbits, only beady pink pupils surrounded by irises like those of a white rabbit suffering from a severe case of conjunctivitis. He frightened the hell out of me!

"After I incapacitate you, I'm going to use one of your dull carving knives and peel you like an onion. You'll be awake or if you should pass-out or decide to take a nap, I'll make sure to wake you so you don't miss out on any of the fun."

"But first I think I'll break your fingers one by one. We're both men of the digital age so it's fitting," he punned before knuckling down. "After stripping your flesh piece by small piece, I'll castrate you to break the monotony. You never had any stones to begin with so no loss. What's the expression, no pain, no gain, as the masochistic pundits like to remind?"

"Finally, I'll drag your pathetic body to the toilet and shove your head in the bowl. I'll put down the lid and sit for awhile so you can think about your miserable life going down the drain. Don't worry. I'll show you glorious Merci! When I'm finished with you, I'll make appointments with Frank and Mary for similar treatment. In Mary's case, I have some very special ideas to caress and fondle her delicious body."

But you won't touch her clit, my friend, I aimlessly and shamelessly thought.

Just as Booku was about to finish his *To Do* list, I bolted for the door. But I didn't get far with the bullet he fired into my left shoulder. I spun around and fell to the floor in excruciating pain. I was quickly going into shock and blood flowed freely from my wound and onto the carpet. Phil would be mightily pissed at my poor housekeeping skills. I'd never hear the end of his bitching—at least I hoped so.

With my remaining strength, I picked up a dining room chair and threw it through the front window. I followed it, rolling through and badly cutting myself in the process. Booku tried to do the same but got caught by my good elbow to his face. With his head posed and poised over the sharp, jagged shards of glass, I pushed it down with all of my might and moved it side-to-side to finish the grisly job. The broken glass severed his jugular vein and he bled out and died a quick death. I thoughtfully closed his eyes because I couldn't stand to look at them. Monsieur Merci Beaucoup had finally met his match and ultimate destiny.

Sitting on the stoop outside my apartment, I lit a Marlboro to calm my jangled nerves. I always enjoyed a good smoke after being fucked-over. I then remembered what this was all about in the final end:

Payback was never a bitch; it was always a Dick as I repetitiously and repeatedly liked to say over and over again until people got my generous point.

Sometimes those who protect and serve could be such a pane in the glass!

AFTERWORD

It's been almost a year since I returned from Liberia. Like me, the country continues to limp along. I have to tell you that I wasn't exactly in the pink because my checkbook was in the red again. I won't admit to being blue but I was quickly heading in that colorful direction. I was still looking for the pot of gold at the end of life's rainbow. My search hadn't gotten me anywhere so far. Maybe my luck and prospecting would change for the better with another assignment from Jersey Briggs.

I hadn't heard from the guy in months. He still must be busy basking in the glory of Booku's death, Ellen Sirleaf's new found moral authority and Liberia's hope for a better future. It was another DS bedtime story that he could pass down orally, aurally and anally to the younger agents. The organization liked happy endings.

President Sirleaf had consolidated more power and was actively pushing through her democratic reforms. Life had gotten marginally better for the people but the verdict was still out as to whether Liberia would survive as a viable nation. She still hadn't decided on running for a second term. She'd likely wet her finger and stick it in the air to test the waters. That's often how decisions and mixed metaphors were made in Liberia.

My grapevine informed me that Mary Tambo had gotten engaged to a prominent Bassa tribesman who had strong political aspirations. She'd decided to stay in Liberia after all. I mentally wished her the best of luck and a long, happy life. She deserved the very best for what she'd endured. She was a good trooper and brave lady and I admired her greatly for her courage.

Frank Yeaten had been promoted to director of the SSS. He had reached the pinnacle of his profession and would be an able administrator. I'd given him Booku's map of all of the rebel munitions caches in the country. I'd found it in Booku's wallet where he'd cleverly sewn it into the lining. I prayed to God that Frank didn't have any visions of Sugar Plum Fairies or bloody coups dancing in his head! Delusions of grandeur weren't necessarily confined to human monsters.

I decided to call Jersey Briggs to see if there were any bones or crumbs he could throw my way. I didn't mind their taste one bit at my age. But it was tough to swallow my pride along with my commonsense. However, I badly needed the money and chance to prove I still had the right stuff. I really wanted to strut it again for my Uncle Sam.

There must be more loathsome barbarians knocking on America's gate. Maybe he'd give me another chance to answer the door.